The Lost Archive

Also by Lynn C. Miller

Novels

The Fool's Journey

Death of a Department Chair

The Day After Death

The Unmasking

Nonfiction

Find Your Story, Write Your Memoir (with Lisa Lenard Cook)

The Lost Archive

LYNN C. MILLER

THE UNIVERSITY OF WISCONSIN PRESS

Publication of this book has been made
possible, in part, through support from the
Brittingham Trust.

The University of Wisconsin Press
728 State Street, Suite 443
Madison, Wisconsin 53706
uwpress.wisc.edu

Gray's Inn House, 127 Clerkenwell Road
London EC1R 5DB, United Kingdom
eurospanbookstore.com

Printed in the United States of America
This book may be available in a digital edition.

Library of Congress Cataloging-in-Publication Data

Names: Miller, Lynn, 1951- author.
Title: The lost archive / Lynn C. Miller.
Description: Madison, Wisconsin : The University of Wisconsin Press, 2023.
Identifiers: LCCN 2022028854 | ISBN 9780299342241 (paperback)
Subjects: LCGFT: Fiction. | Short stories.
Classification: LCC PS3613.I544 L67 2023 | DDC 813/.6—dc23/eng/20220916
LC record available at https://lccn.loc.gov/2022028854

For
LYNDA

In a sense we all are crashing to our death from the top story of our birth to the flat stones of the churchyard and wondering with an immortal Alice in Wonderland at the patterns of the passing wall.

—VLADIMIR NABOKOV

Contents

EXHIBIT A

Archival Footage 3

How Much Is Enough? 10

Afterthought 19

Pueblo Luna 27

Words Shimmer 31

EXHIBIT B

Is It Really You? 45

Duluth 52

David's Harvest 56

Coincidence 72

Other Married People 75

How Did You Know It Was Time to Go? 79

EXHIBIT C

Pale Blue 93

Standing in the Light 98

Curiosities 102

Noir by Night 112

Everyday Monsters 116

Regret 121

EXHIBIT D

Old Vines   129

Flight   136

Dry Tinder   140

The Dead Know   145

The Last Usher   149

Acknowledgments   171

The Lost
Archive

EXHIBIT A

Archival Footage

Here we go down the rabbit hole again, Audra thought as she unpacked several boxes of manuscripts over a hundred years old. The university research library where she worked had recently acquired a rare cache of a reclusive woman writer's papers, much of it fragile. This sensation of diving down into the unknown struck her every time she dug into a new acquisition and passed through the doorway into another world. She often emerged in a stupor, dazed as if from time travel, wondering where she might be. Submerged in other lives and other times, the journey through each archive changed her. Sometimes she feared there was no going back.

In college studying library science, Audra had immersed herself in archives as she interned at a well-known research center for twentieth-century writers. She liked placing old letters in their transparent, protective wrappers, sorting through boxes of rare manuscripts, poring over early drafts of someone's masterpiece. An archive was a repository of materials that opened a window into a life. But then one day it occurred to her how archives were in the end just a convenient way of ordering things. In fact, memory itself was an archive. Who you were depended upon what—and how—you remembered. Each day, material got added. Other details dropped away from lack of use.

The idea obsessed her. She began making lists. First the ten most important things that had ever happened to her, then the fifteen most memorable. When that wasn't enough, she taped big sheets of paper together and placed the huge rectangle on the ground, making outlines about these events, adding details, so that the paper looked like a forest of Edward Gorey trees, little lines of print extending out in spidery waves.

A Lewis Carroll commemorative exhibition mounted at the library suddenly took on new meaning for Audra. The rabbit hole became personal, an opening that dropped you into a place that once made up your life, or your ancestor's life, or somewhere that you dreamed. And each world led to another as you ventured further into the labyrinth of possibility. Or, sometimes, limitation.

She became so fixated on this idea that she mentioned it to her friend Haley at lunch. "So, you see," she concluded at the end of a long speech about what she was now calling *memory as archive*, "every single person is unconsciously making these selections all of the time, remembering certain details that lead to others."

Haley carefully placed a crust of baguette at the side of her plate. As she thought, she scrunched her forehead in a way Audra had always found endearing. "Okay, the outline of this makes some sense. But I'm not sure I get it." The skin around her eyes crinkled. "So . . . our friendship is an archive?"

"Yes! But my archive of our lives together may be completely different from yours. Here's a for instance: remember my tenth birthday party? It looms in my memory as horrible because one of my best friends, Carol, came to the party, made a face at me, threw her present in my face, and made her mother take her home. It ruined the whole party. I felt like such a failure. You were there—do you remember Carol doing that?"

"Um, no," Haley said, pushing her wavy dark hair away from her face. "I guess that whole episode did not get stored in my archive of being ten at all. Huh," she said. "I'm beginning to get this. So, for you, you went down the rabbit hole of embarrassment and misery because Carol, whose last name is not in my archive either, made you feel insignificant. Like shit. It's like Alice drinking the potion that shrank her into a tiny person." Beginning to get excited, Haley began to talk faster. "You lost your confidence. The world became a huge scary place!"

"Well, I don't know if I'd go quite that far," Audra said. "I mean, it didn't ruin my life or anything."

"Maybe not, but that day made it into your archive!" Haley finished, a radiant smile on her face.

At first, Audra realized she was protective of her idea about archive and memory and wished she hadn't mentioned it to Haley at all. Haley was a clinical psychologist. For years Audra had heard stories about her struggling patients—not by name, of course, that would break a professional boundary. But then Audra sensed that she had forged another bond with Haley. She herself heard thoughts and voices coming through the archives she studied just as Haley teased out the inner voices of her clients.

The two usually had lunch every two weeks. Both forty, they had met in first grade and so had known each other thirty-four years. Audra didn't have other friends who went that far back. As an only child and newly single with both parents gone—she still very much missed her mother, who had died over a year ago—this shared history gave her comfort. Audra had cousins, but she saw them only occasionally. Haley was a touchstone for her in many ways.

Touchstone. That concept might be important to the idea of archive too. Alice in Wonderland had touchstones: the White Rabbit himself, who kept scurrying, worrying about being late; the elusive glorious Cheshire Cat, parts of his body materializing and dissolving in front of Alice; the Mad Hatter and his tea party. The Cheshire Cat told Alice that the world was mad. When she objected that *she* wasn't, he said of course that since she was part of the mad world, that made her mad, too. Even the potion Alice drank was a sort of touchstone. It shaped how the girl perceived the world, from the vantage point of her original height where objects and people seemed in balance to her, to when she grew to an extreme height that dwarfed all that was around her, or when she shrank to a tiny being at the whims of others. When Alice was very small, a normal-size person sobbing could create a river of tears that might sweep her off her feet and out to sea.

Audra sometimes felt out to sea as she worked in the library, cataloging the accumulation of documents of writers like T. S. Eliot or Edith Wharton. She read pieces of their lives, trying to place herself in their time and place. Wharton had a love diary, very private, that she never wanted published; it later became part of Yale University's archive. Then there were the letters to her lover, Morton Fullerton, which she also assumed would be private. And yet here the letters were, at the research center where Audra worked, found by a graduate student in a trove of papers. When she submerged herself in the letters, which showed a woman desperately in love with a man unworthy of her, Audra lost track of the expansive life of the great novelist, her ambition and achievement, her worldliness. She concluded that Wharton was correct in wishing to guard access to her inner life. An archive could be misleading.

One afternoon she and Haley packed a lunch and went on a hike into the mountains. In a saddle of the Sandia Mountains, they looked down at Albuquerque, the blue sky sharp and clear around them.

"I've been thinking about your fascination with the archive," Haley said, although Audra had very carefully said nothing about it for at least two months.

"Oh?" Audra picked up a carrot slice. "It's just an idea."

"Well, I think you have something there. What if this really is the key to relationships, for example?" Haley often saw people for couples counseling. "Maybe what makes relationships founder is that the details in the history of a marriage, for example, start to diverge widely. What if the things that are precious memories for one person become just a big blank to the other? The relational archive, what both people cherish or just find memorable, gets emptier and emptier."

Audra found herself hollowed out by this thought. Was this the horror of living with someone with dementia, the memories of the marriage, a strong glue, beginning to weaken and then to disintegrate?

"That makes sense to me," Audra said slowly. She folded a piece of paper towel into a smaller and smaller square. "Who are we if we don't share the past?" She thought a moment. "I do think that people divorce not just to leave a person behind but to leave their old selves behind."

She and her partner, Sandra, had separated for just that reason. They had met at thirty-one and by age thirty-nine, had drifted apart in search of the next phase of their lives. Audra had been unhappy about this, but eventually saw that they were both evolving into different people—were they to meet now, they would most likely not choose to connect.

Haley looked stricken for a moment. Audra wondered if she was thinking of her own two divorces until Haley leaped in with: "We've been friends forever. Tell me what is one really, *really* important memory you have that involves the two of us."

The question unnerved Audra. Was Haley fishing for a story that glorified her value? She hoped that Haley didn't doubt that she was important to Audra. She hesitated to say anything; what if what was important to her didn't matter to Haley? Might this strain their friendship?

"Well, one memory is when we went to London right after we graduated from college. You argued with me about the names of the ducks in Hyde Park. That sticks in my mind for some reason. We loved rummaging around Bloomsbury—the British Museum, the bookshops." She laughed. "I remember being terrified that our shoes wouldn't be nice enough to go to the Palm Court for tea. Silly detail, I guess."

Haley frowned. "I'd forgotten the Ritz tearoom. What I remember is how you'd arranged to meet a friend later to take the train to Scotland and how abandoned I felt."

"Oh. I'm pretty sure we invited you to come along." Audra's mood slumped. Haley never forgot a slight, or in this case a perceived slight.

"I don't think so." Haley squinted up at the sky. "I think those are rain clouds. We'd better get off the mountain."

As they scrambled through some scrub oak, then onto their trail, Audra offered, "The trip to London was your idea, and it was a really good one."

"Mmmm," Haley responded, then sped ahead of Audra down the steep slope.

Haley's impulse to put herself at the center of the archive of their friendship led Audra to a central fact. An archive usually focused on a single famous person. It was not impartial or necessarily expansive or illuminating. Like memories, the documents or incidents radiated outward like the web spun by a spider at its center. A record of connections, intriguing meetings, or random jottings, the archive—like memory—represented prime moments. Together all the materials bolstered the frail ego of the person collecting them.

An archive made one seem larger than life. How then was it different from the accumulation of wealth, say, or things acquired that shielded many people from their mortality? After Audra's mother died, when Audra cleaned out her house, she had found that parting with any of her possessions had been wrenching. Each piece of furniture, her clothes, treasured pieces of pottery and art, all had seemed to insulate her mother when she had been alive. Now these objects expanded her presence beyond herself.

Audra's mother had not been able to get pregnant until her early forties. She and Audra's father, who was ten years older, had been delighted to have a daughter. At various times in her life Audra noticed how her mother had labored over her piles of scrapbooks, compiling notes about ancestors and their immigration to America, leaving an account behind for the next generation, for Audra and for the children of her mother's sisters, so that she wouldn't disappear.

Audra appreciated all these leavings when her mother died at the age of eighty-six. But she liked to think that many other things lived on about her mother, elusive things like her touch and smell, the young girl sound of her laughter, her way of spontaneously sashaying around the kitchen—often leading Audra along with her as they glided across the floor, occasionally bumping into cabinets—when she cooked. These moments lived on in the archive about her mother Audra had been building all of her conscious life.

On the second anniversary of her mother's death, Audra stayed home from work. She collected all the letters and memorabilia, the scrapbooks, the scads of photos, and her own diary jottings about her mother. Sitting in the middle of the floor, she spread these things around her, including a black mesh evening bag, very 1940s, which she had kept when she cleaned out her mother's house.

Because of her father's long stint abroad in military service during their courtship, her parents had been separated for almost a year before marrying. Audra opened a pile of letters her mother had saved during those long months. *My dearest Dorothy, I miss every inch of your beautiful self . . . I hear your voice echoing through your letters, warm, earnest . . . if only you were laughing right beside me. . . .* Audra had never seen this tender side of her father. She felt like an interloper witnessing his youthful longing. As a teenager, Audra had often been embarrassed by her parents' obvious affection for each other. Now, holding this proof in her hands, she realized how lucky they had been. Like a musical score, the notes sang with sound and feeling.

She was touched by clippings her mother had saved about her daughter's high school achievements, roles in school plays, editorship of the yearbook, the award as best all-around student in her senior year. Who now cared about this young Audra as her mother had, lovingly building the record of the daughter in whom she had placed so many hopes and ambitions? Audra realized that a part of her own life had disappeared when her mother died.

Reaching for the teenage diaries that recorded her agony at her parents' stodginess, as she labeled it then, she found she had no appetite for reading them. Not now, surrounded by the vivid presence of the mother she had come to treasure. Instead, she put aside a few of her mother's notes and clippings to show Haley. Her friend had loved Audra's mother, fascinated by stories of Dorothy's wide-ranging travels after the isolation of growing up on a farm in Wisconsin. The three of them played cards and board games together in the late afternoons after she and Haley got out of school.

Audra remembered Haley and Dorothy throwing their arms in the air during rummy games. "I'm out!" one of them would crow while the other giggled and mock-threatened, "Just wait . . ." When Haley was nine, she had looked around the table with her pixie smile: "Three's not a crowd. It's a perfect circle."

Haley had more than once told Audra in the last year what a wonderful companion she had found Dorothy to be. Audra now recognized that her mother had been just that: lively, attentive, and funny, engaged by others but not allowing herself to be swallowed up by them.

Absorbing the many photographs and letters, Audra scanned party invitations and concert programs, the papers dry and brittle in their plastic sleeves. She held her mother's much-loved garnet ring in her palm and then slipped it onto her right hand. The stone radiated warmth and comfort. It settled so comfortably onto her finger that her hand seemed fuller and stronger. She heard her mother's approval in her mind: *All right then.*

The hours passed; the day darkened outside the windows. Audra felt contained as the archive deepened around her. Alive, shifting like the desert sands, it seemed at times too hot to touch, at others reshaping the imprints of what had gone before.

Audra sensed the edges of her life lapping against the edges of those of her family, her friends, and all the lives she had touched, one archive leading to another, interspersing into a giant tapestry of living, striving, dreaming.

How Much Is Enough?

Janene's fingers itched to tear into the envelope her neighbor Steve handed over as they stood on her front porch. The tangled scrawl of her address—half cursive, half print—belonged to Nathan, her ex.

Steve took off his cap to reveal curly dark hair. "This came to my mailbox, but it's yours," he said.

"Oh, thanks, Steve." Steve was always helping everyone on the block—clearing leaves out of gutters, changing out locks for the perpetually keyless, mowing the lawn of their elderly neighbors.

Steve stood there, perhaps hoping to be invited inside for a cup of coffee.

"I'd ask you in, but I have a doctor's appointment in an hour and as you can see, I'm not ready," Janene improvised, pointing at her paint-stained sweatpants.

"Hope you're okay," Steve said, resting his hands on his hips.

"Just routine. Thanks a lot for bringing this." Janene waved and stepped back into the doorway, closing the door on Steve's smile.

Janene ripped the narrow edge off the envelope and slid out a single sheet of paper. She hadn't had word one from Nathan in what, two years? Sitting at the kitchen table, feet flat on the floor, she unfolded the page. *Janene, I'll bet you'll be surprised hearing from me. I'm kinda surprised too. Things ended for us with a . . . well, let's say they for sure ended. But I'm coming to Albuquerque in April for a training, and I'd really like to see you. On April 18. Let me know if you have time for a cup of coffee.* He had scribbled his name and a phone number at the end.

Janene let the paper drop. It drifted to the floor and landed faceup. Damn. She had moved, changed her cell number, quit her old job, and started her own business, all to make sure Nathan would not be able to get in touch when he got out of prison last year. So, how did he get her address?

Her stomach clenched. She needed coffee, with lots of milk and sugar. She threw a cartridge into her coffeemaker, poured some milk to heat in the microwave. It wasn't that she was afraid of Nathan. Not really. He had embezzled funds from a construction company—Nathan was an accountant—which is why he had been convicted to begin with. He hadn't hurt anyone really—well, not in a physical way.

The microwave dinged. There she went again, making excuses for the man! Of course he had hurt people. What about that company that couldn't meet its payroll back in 2010 because of Nathan? She fumed as she slid the full cup from the machine and poured in milk. The coffee's caramel swirl reassured her. She rummaged in the refrigerator for a bran muffin, taking it and the coffee into the living room.

April 18. She checked her phone. Next week. She didn't have to answer, of course, but the thing is, the man knew where she lived.

The next day, she called Nathan's number, leaving a message to say she would meet him at the coffee shop on Central by the old Otero's men's shop, now a shoe store. She had always been sad old man Otero retired. She missed looking in the windows at the beautiful suits on the manikins with the fine scarves folded under the lapels. On their second anniversary, she bought one of those suits for Nathan.

She had had to call Nathan, even though it meant now he had her cell number as well as her address. She couldn't have him in her house. Not in the space that was entirely hers for the first time in her life. She had met Nathan after graduating from college and moved directly from a house with three roommates into an apartment with him. Three years later, they married and bought their first house. This was the first time she had lived alone. She wanted to keep it that way.

The days passed slowly. She worked as a freelance editor, and the book she was working on was in its fourth rewrite. The author, a repeat client of hers, always had great ideas but poor execution. She wondered if that reflected badly on her own skills—but she wasn't the man's teacher, for chrissakes. It wasn't her fault that he didn't seem to get any better as a writer.

On April 18, she drove downtown to the coffee shop, the Liquid Bean. As usual, a few scattered people read papers or worked on their laptops. Three women in late middle age leaned in toward each other, engaged in serious conversation. Janene ordered a double latte, then chose a table in the corner.

At exactly 3:00 p.m., Nathan arrived. Funny how prompt he was, how precise he was about numbers and time, things that she supposed came in handy for accountants in general and embezzlers in particular.

She waved as he stepped into the café, his handsome face creased in a smile, his dark brown hair still full though streaked with gray at the crown. His overcoat was camel colored. Cashmere? He looked prosperous and healthy, very little changed from the last time she had seen him.

He came toward her. Should they hug? Shake hands? She didn't stand up but extended her hand. He grasped it and leaned down, resting his face against hers for a long moment.

"You're looking well," she said. *Not at all like someone who's been in prison*, she was thinking, even though he had left there over a year ago. She searched his face; it looked untroubled and serene.

She gestured at the seat opposite her, and he took it.

"You look terrific," he said. His eyes sweeping across her face looked a bit hungry. Or was she imagining it?

"Um, how about I get you a coffee?" she offered.

To her surprise, he said, "Okay. Make it an espresso. Double." The old Nathan was always getting her things, opening car doors, making spaghetti dinners. This one snuggled down into his chair, his legs comfortably crossed. The foot in the air made slow circles.

"Thanks, Janene." He accepted the cup from her when she returned.

Tipping the cup, he took a long swallow. The Bean's coffee was scalding. She felt like she was watching a sword swallower.

"Love it hot," he explained. "Ever since I was inside. Coffee, soup, you name it—everything was always lukewarm." He looked around the room with a contented smile.

Janene made a show of glancing at her watch. Where was this headed? "What—"

"I suppose you'd like—" Nathan said at the same time.

They both stopped, sipped at their coffees.

"You first." Uneasy, Janene waited. The problem was, Nathan was so damn attractive. And she hadn't met anybody else. Not that she wanted to, she reminded herself. She steeled herself—saying no to him had always been hard.

He swept his hands in front of him with a "let's put our cards on the table" motion. "It's about our house."

Hearing how casually he appropriated her house, Janene flushed. "You mean my house, the one I live in?"

His voice was steady. "That's our house, Janene. You sold our 'old' house. I paid for at least half of that house, and then you bought a new house. With my money as well as yours. So, our house."

"When you left, you left me with the mortgage and three credit cards that were maxed out. I paid off the cards, and I covered the mortgage until I sold it." She blinked rapidly, remembering those months of having to scrape together every dollar for the house payment and the utility bills. She had felt forced to sell their house in the end and downsize. "It was damn hard for a long time."

"I really appreciate that, Janene."

The repetition of her name in Nathan's pleasant baritone irked her. "It was the right thing to do. And it was my credit at risk as much as yours."

Neither of them mentioned that in his case having a felony on your record didn't exactly help your credit rating.

"We're separated," she said. "And you must know I've filed for divorce."

"Apparently you don't have my correct address. I don't know anything about it."

Janene knew her lawyer had sent out the divorce papers a week before Nathan's letter reached her. Coincidence? Not a chance. Her mouth trembled as she tried to keep her expression neutral. Damned if she would let this man see how his words were like . . . like being smacked in the head when you were just walking along on a sunny day admiring the view. She heard her father's voice in her head: "The *gall* of that SOB . . ." Her father had never liked Nathan. When he had been convicted, her dad had taken her by the shoulders with his strong, big-knuckled hands and said, "You are so much better than he is. You don't even know the half of it."

She had been too stunned to ask him to explain what the whole of it might be. "Thanks, Dad," she had whispered. Two years ago, when she stood in the cemetery at his graveside service, she had thrown a red rose onto his coffin. "Thanks, Dad," she had said again, tears welling up. "For having my back. Always." After he was gone, she felt like she had lost the love of her life.

She pushed her coffee cup away from her, placed her hands on the table. "Nathan, when you first went away, I wrote you almost every day, asking you how you wanted me to deal with our financial affairs. You didn't answer. Then, if you remember, after the first month, you refused to see me. You knew how much money I was making. Thank God my dad helped me, or I don't know what I'd have done."

"You look like you're doing pretty well for yourself," he said. She saw those hungry eyes again.

"I could say the same about you. My consulting work is doing better. And I've had an offer from an advertising company if I want a steady paycheck and more structure." Looking at Nathan, Janene was pretty sure she needed structure. "I have a life now, Nathan, and I like it."

"Look, about turning you away back then . . . I didn't want you to see me the way I was. I was embarrassed. Mortified." The skin over his cheekbones looked mottled. "I didn't want you to see me all . . . washed-up."

Janene felt short of breath. "I know you have some money socked away. You told me that yourself when you knew you were going to be arrested. 'They won't find it, Janene,' you said. 'Don't worry about a thing. Especially the house. I can cover it.' That was the last I heard about it."

He nodded slowly as if considering a weighty question. "Well, when I found out I had to do three years, three fucking unbearably long years I might add, I had to have a stake when I came out. I didn't know if you'd ever talk to me again."

Janene rose, light-headed, realizing that she had chosen to meet him instead of ignoring his note. "I have to go."

"But wait, Janene. Let me explain. I have a proposal for you." He added quickly, "You don't know how much you mean to me, how much I care about you. I worked hard for you always, you know that."

"Is that what you said to the people you worked with when you stole their money?" she blurted out.

His eyes, large and gray, were pleading now. "Please, just five more minutes."

Janene's knees felt wobbly. She sat back down. "Okay. Five. This better be good."

Nathan grinned. "That sounds like a line from a movie."

Incredulous, she was silent. Then, "This is not a movie, Nathan. The clock is ticking. And don't say it, I know that sounds like a line from a movie too." Anger made her voice crisp. "Because that's how people talk. Normal people. Movies are written that way on purpose."

Nathan grinned again, a charming lopsided grin. He should have been an actor. Hell, he was an actor!

She stared at her watch. "Four minutes."

"Hey," he reached for her hand. She clasped her fingers together and shook her head.

He huffed out a sigh, buttoned and then unbuttoned one of his jacket buttons. "So, here's what I propose." He held up a hand like a stop sign. "Don't say a word until you hear me out. Please."

She waited and then nodded.

"I did have some money. But I've been out for a year and that money's gone. But I want to start a new accounting business. I—"

"I can't imagine you can get back into accounting, Nathan, not after what you did—"

"You said you'd hear me out." His voice sounded under pressure. She imagined a tire filled almost to bursting.

Janene clamped her lips together and tried to keep her face neutral. When her husband had been convicted, she had lost all confidence in herself. What kind of a choice had she made? What was she doing with her life?

"I'm hoping you'll let me move back in, just until I get my feet back under me."

Janene's nerves jolted, like she had been stung. She must have missed something. "What? I told you I've filed for divorce."

"But we're not divorced. Not yet. You owe me half of what the house is worth, Janene."

She couldn't help herself, she laughed. "That's your proposal? After I paid off forty thousand dollars on your credit cards? That I share my house with you? I crawled out of a big hole when you left, Nathan. And I did it without your help." She clutched her purse to her chest. Her heart actually hurt, a deep aching pain blooming under her sternum. This man was not good for her health.

Nathan turned his head and looked at the bakery case at the front of the coffee shop, as if searching for a new angle, a bit of sugar to sweeten the deal he was offering. But when he turned back to her, he gave her a tight smile. "Then sell the house. And give me my half."

The words *sell the house* echoed in her brain. As if it was merely a signature line on a form, not a place she belonged, a place where she had sanded floors and built cabinets and chosen paint colors in soothing shades of green. A refuge.

Pain bloomed in the back of her head. Nathan's cashmere coat mocked her. He had always been a charmer. And a good lover. Now she wondered if she had just been holding air.

She squinted at him, wanting a clear view, no going back. A reckless anger flooded her throat, and her chin jutted forward as she said too loudly, "Okay, you're a gambler. So, let's just go for broke. Do you want our marriage back, or do you just want the house?"

She waited. Nathan stared at her, his gray eyes narrowed. They sat that way for at least two minutes.

Then, he picked up his briefcase from the floor and drew out a stack of papers. "I just happen to have an agreement about the house with me," he said.

The papers, neatly arranged in front of Nathan's chest, blended in with his white shirt, until everything blurred in front of her. She blinked rapidly. Then a choking laugh erupted from her throat and her eyes watered. She scrambled in her purse, the one she still clutched for dear life, and swiped at her face with a tissue.

"I don't think so," she finally managed. "I'm not much for gambling. But it's good to try it once in a while. Just to find out where you stand." A part of her was very rational—*he doesn't give a shit about you, Janene*—while the rest of her rocked between hurt and fury.

The broad planes of Nathan's face stiffened. "You weren't serious?"

She breathed in, held the breath for four counts, then expelled it. The room steadied. "It isn't really a good idea to tell a woman to her face that you'd prefer cash to her company, thank you very much."

"You've changed," he said, sweeping the papers back into the briefcase, snapping the lock closed with a satisfying click. "You tricked me. You never wanted our marriage back, did you?" Almost as an afterthought, he said, "You really won't sign the agreement?"

Janene lowered her purse, straightened her back, finally confident she had made the right move. "No," she said. "But I'll tell you what I will do. When you have a business that's . . . let's say, *viable*—isn't that what you accountants like to say?—we'll go to a lawyer and I'll put up twenty percent of the capital. You'll give me twenty-five percent of the profits each year. And when that adds up to what I paid on your credit cards and makes up for the loss on our house that I had to sell when the market was down, we'll call it even. And we'll be done."

There was a silence. "You're kidding," Nathan said. "You don't want to share your house with me, you want a divorce in fact, but you'll invest in my business? After you've basically told me no one will ever trust me again?" He threw his eyes heavenward. "We'll be even? How does that help me?"

"It doesn't. But it really does. Because then I won't go after you, Nathan. Because you see, if we sell the house, *my* house, by the time the mortgage is paid off, there won't be even half the amount of money I'm talking about, the money I spent to bail you out. You won't have to pay me back this way. I've already paid you more than your half was worth. Don't you see that?"

"All I see is that you must hate me." Nathan's face, usually marked by the flush of health, was drained of all color. He unbuttoned his collar, lengthened his tie.

Janene felt too much to feel at all. She swayed back on her heels. Finally, she spoke just above a whisper: "I don't hate you. But I can't live with you. Someday you'll see I've been your friend. Someone who has never, ever tried to take advantage of you. Someone who never claimed what wasn't rightfully mine."

She stood up and noticed Nathan's thick hair, hair she had once loved to run her hands through. It looked tarnished. "I'm going to go now," she said. "My lawyer will be in touch with you."

"Janene . . ."

"I'm sure we'll talk again. Someday." She hitched her bag over her shoulder. "You have a lot, Nathan. Your looks, your health. And your dreams."

Saying that made her feel a lot better. Now she needed to do something physical. Maybe she would go home and take her neighbor Steve up on his offer to help her clean out the rain gutters on her house. It struck her that Steve's nose in profile looked a bit like her father's.

Her husband—she already found herself thinking, her *former* husband—broke into her reverie by saying in a wary voice: "My dreams?"

"I know you. You've always had big ideas. One of them will work out, you'll see."

As she made her way toward the door, she thought she would take that job with the advertising firm. They had promised her a partnership in just two years. It was time to stretch a little, reach beyond the low-hanging fruit, as her father had liked to call it.

Janene remembered hiking with her dad up the east side of the Sandia Mountains one autumn day. The aspens were turning yellow, and the trail wound through the trees, curving upward toward the sky. On a day like that, the air cool and the sun warm, the light bathing the mountains in a soft gold, anything seemed possible.

Afterthought

Ingrid hoped she wasn't too late.

She stepped up to the uneven stoop of the diner, pulled down the short jacket she wore with her denim skirt, and opened the door. Somewhere in the back, a bell tinkled. The sound of the bell made her feel twelve years old again, during those days when she helped her uncle in this place, when she still lived in Jamestown, North Dakota.

Across the room an old street sign hung from the ceiling: *Sixth and Main*. On the walls were bulletin boards brimming with photos and quotations. These had been there when she had helped Uncle Jay too—twenty years ago. She went over to a booth and leaned close to the wall where she recognized the Eiffel Tower and the Grand Canyon. A saying of Mark Twain's was written in her uncle's neat cursive and placed in the middle of the board: "Truth is more of a stranger than fiction."

An elderly man came through the curtain from the back, wiping his hands on a towel. The skin hung on his big frame as if the flesh had suddenly melted away. "We don't open for another forty-five minutes, not 'til eleven. But if you want you can . . ."

He stuck his neck forward, a turtle testing the air. "Ingrid? Oh my God, Ingrid!" He tossed the towel on the bar that separated the booths and tables from the food preparation area and held out his arms as he hurried toward her. Ingrid noticed he was limping. Uncle Jay had been a star runner in college, coached the boys' little league team for years and years. He had been ageless. Until now.

Ingrid clutched her purse with one hand and hugged her uncle close with the other arm.

"Oh, honey," he said. "I was afraid you wouldn't hear the news in time."

Ingrid had been traveling overseas for ten years, teaching English to American children of servicepeople in South Korea and Germany. Then she had spent a year in Stockholm working at a small hotel as a desk clerk while she wrote the play she had been trying to write since she had graduated from college. She had visited only infrequently during this time but managed to return every two or three years.

"I'm so sorry, Uncle Jay. About Aunt Rachel." She gave him an extra squeeze before she let him go. The two of them had basically raised her. They had taken her in when her own parents died. Their car had rolled over in a rainstorm when she was in junior high.

She looked up and was startled to see her uncle's face frozen in a kind of grimace when she had expected tears. He absently patted her shoulder. "Your aunt wasn't herself at the end. You wouldn't have known her." His face didn't thaw.

A wave of unease swept through Ingrid. Her aunt had suffered from dementia for several years, but she had assumed her uncle had been caring for her with his typical patience and devotion. From his letters, Uncle Jay had managed to run his business, scheduling caregivers for daily walks when Aunt Rachel became unable to find her way back from long rambles in the woods in the city park near their house, doing the shopping, and preparing meals. An old family friend pruned Rachel's prize yellow roses while she slept in a chair on the porch.

"I'm so sorry I wasn't here to help you, Uncle Jay." She tried to engage his eyes, but he was staring at a spot on the marbled Formica tabletop of the booth off to the side of him. He began to rub the spot in a hypnotic circular motion.

"What happened?" Ingrid took her uncle's hand. "Can you sit with me a minute?" She waited. "You're looking kind of pale. Are you okay? Let me get you a glass of water."

She bustled behind the bar, retrieved a glass, filled it, and fished a chocolate chip cookie out of a jar. Her uncle had low blood sugar. Something was very wrong. Her aunt's funeral was tomorrow, and Jay didn't seem to know what day it was.

Guiding her uncle into the booth that he had been so obsessively focused on, she put the water in front of him. She pulled a paper napkin out of the dispenser on the table, placed it under the cookie, and slid it next to the water. She sat opposite him.

"Did she just start to fail?" Her face grew hot. She needed to start over—Aunt Rachel had *been* failing. That was a fact. "I know Aunt Rachel wasn't doing so well the last couple of years, but she seemed pretty stable . . ."

She broke off as she sat across from him. "If you don't mind talking about it," she added.

Jay shuddered, as if he had been asleep and then jolted awake into that zone of not knowing where he was. "She was stable. For a long time." He passed a trembling hand through his thin ginger hair. "Gosh, I don't think you've been home for . . . I don't know when was the last time . . ."

"Two years." Ingrid spoke gently but regret pierced her intensely, as if pinning her to the back of the booth. She squirmed against the red vinyl.

Her uncle's lips trembled. "I'm trying to remember how she was then."

"Good. She was good." Ingrid nodded too eagerly. "She knew me. Remember we played Monopoly?"

"Yeah, Rach loved games. Always used to beat me." His face lifted in a crooked smile. "I had to quit playing Scrabble with her because she never let me win. Not one game."

"So, she seemed fine when I visited last," Ingrid prompted.

Uncle Jay nibbled on the cookie. He chewed for a long time. "You didn't know her family very well, but she had three sisters, all of them much older than she was. She was almost another generation, an afterthought as we used to say. Each in her turn got dementia in their early eighties—in the old days we used to call it senility. What they had was the damnedest thing because it didn't really progress much. The oldest sister lived to be ninety-six, stayed in bed the last eight years. Wasn't Alzheimer's. No organ failure or anything like that."

He stared past Ingrid, shook his head. "Rachel just went down slowly, lived more and more in the past, kept asking for her parents and sisters, slept most of the time."

Ingrid nodded encouragingly. "You thought at first Aunt Rachel wasn't changing much, that she was just getting a little forgetful maybe?"

"She only lived to be seventy-eight. It wasn't her time!" Jay's mouth drew into a thin line. Then he nodded. "She faded. A day at a time, she left me. You can't imagine what that was like. She was disappearing right in front of me, getting farther and farther out of reach, and I was running after trying to catch her. And I couldn't." His voice broke as his face dissolved into bafflement. "There was only Rachel for me. She was the only woman I ever loved. I would've done anything for her. Why didn't it happen to me?"

Ingrid wasn't sure what he meant. Did he mean he wished he had lost his memory too so that it all wouldn't be so painful? But then who would have taken care of the two of them? "You didn't want her to leave, ever," she said, trying to understand. She ached to touch her uncle's face and smooth out the crumpled skin. He was trying to tell her something, though, and she didn't want to interrupt him.

"It was so lonely," he said. "She was there and not there, you know?"

"Oh, Uncle Jay." She took his hand which lay limply on the surface of the booth. "I wish I could've done something."

His voice hardened. "No one could do anything. At the end she couldn't walk, couldn't eat, and finally she couldn't talk. You remember her voice, so clear and low and beautiful. Losing that was the hardest thing of all." He pulled his hand away and let it fall to his lap.

Tears were streaming down his craggy face. "But she made me promise, while she still could talk." He was whispering now. "She begged me."

He stopped, shook his head, took a sip of water. He cleared his throat. "I didn't know what to do."

"What did she make you promise?" Ingrid's mouth was dry. She was terrified by what she might hear, but she had to ask.

"That I wouldn't leave her."

"Of course you wouldn't leave her, you—"

"No," he interrupted. "That I wouldn't leave her—as in leave her to get any worse. Every once in a while she woke up, you see, like from a dream. And then she would be almost herself again. Lucid. Competent. And then suddenly, not. It kept me off-balance. I waited for the Rachel I knew to come back." He lifted his glasses and scrubbed at his eyes.

When he didn't say more, Ingrid slumped against the red cushions of the booth. She didn't need her uncle to say any more. Somehow, he had helped Rachel leave this world. That could be the only reason he had that frozen look, in spite of his tears.

"I would've done the same thing," she whispered. "I hope you don't blame yourself."

Uncle Jay's head snapped up on his slender neck. "I'm not sure what you mean."

Without thinking, Ingrid took a sip of her uncle's water. "Um. Whatever happened with Aunt Rachel, it's not your fault, that's all. However you handled things in such a terrible time, I mean." The too-warm room was claustrophobic. "I . . . I don't know what I would have done if I thought she . . ." What could she say? *That if someone I loved so dearly became someone else and begged me to release her I would do it?*

He was watching her narrowly. "In the end her heart just gave up, that's all. I guess it was a blessing." He lowered his eyes and seemed to be waiting.

Ingrid didn't believe heart failure was the whole truth of it. "Did she have hospice?" She spoke slowly, hoping to stumble on the words that might unlock the key to her uncle's mysterious reticence.

He nodded. "Came every day." And then he mumbled under his breath, "Thank the Lord. She was very agitated at the end."

"I've heard that's very common." Imagining her uncle's agony during her aunt's decline, Ingrid twisted the strap of her purse in her fingers. She fought to keep her voice level. "So unlike Aunt Rachel, though."

Why had she stayed away so long? She had known her uncle and aunt were struggling. A cold swell of guilt pressed the air from her lungs. They never had abandoned her as she just had the last two years. Not once.

"I wish you'd been here," Uncle Jay said simply. "I didn't know what to do by myself." His eyes suddenly looked naked and frightened.

The vinyl of the booth was hot and sticky on her bare legs. She half rose and tugged at the hem of her skirt. What had she been doing that was so important when the people she loved needed her? The time had rushed through her fingers like water and now it was gone forever. A terrible thirst seized her.

"I have to get something to drink. Can I get you more water?" She rushed behind the bar and filled up a malted-milk-size glass with lemonade. She passed a hand over the back of her neck; the skin was clammy with sweat. She gulped half a glass of the lemonade and leaned on the bar until a sudden dizziness passed.

"Ice. I could use some ice," Uncle Jay said, his voice fading.

She turned so abruptly that lemonade splashed onto her skirt. "Are you all right?"

Uncle Jay leaned forward over the table as if he had stomach cramps. He was groaning.

Ingrid grabbed a clean cloth from the drawer next to the sink and packed it with ice cubes from the soda dispenser. She ran back to Jay and pressed the compress to the back of his neck. With trembling hands, he took the cloth and passed it over his face, then held it to his forehead.

"Have you been eating enough?" she asked anxiously.

His eyes clouded. "I don't know."

"Well, did you eat breakfast?"

When he shook his head, Ingrid got up. "How about some eggs and toast?"

Jay looked anxiously at the clock on the wall; it read 10:35. "I don't think I have time."

"Of course you do. You have to take care of yourself. What'll it be?"

"Oh, just a piece of toast will be fine."

"With peanut butter, then," Ingrid said. She went to the freezer and found the whole wheat bread with seeds that her uncle always kept there because Aunt Rachel liked it. Sliding it into the toaster oven, she dug the peanut butter and honey from the back of a shelf. When the toast was ready, she placed it on a plate and spread the peanut butter on thick and drizzled the honey over it in a figure eight. She had seen Jay do that on countless mornings.

"Are you in any pain?" Ingrid pointed at his stomach as she put the plate in front of him.

"Yes," he whispered. "Everything hurts." He took a bite of the toast and another sip of water.

Alarmed, Ingrid took out her phone. "I'm calling your doctor."

"A doctor can't fix it. Don't call." He chewed another bite out of duty rather than hunger.

"You're in no shape to work today," she said. "I'm going to put out the *Closed* sign. Or you go in the back room, and I'll serve the lunch today. Why isn't Dotty here?" Dotty had worked for Jay and Rachel for twenty years.

"Sick dog."

Ingrid was about to say something on the order of *This is ridiculous, we're closing!* Or: *Your wife just died. And you can't do this without Dotty anyhow!* But before she could speak, Jay said, "You know Rachel thought of you as her daughter. Hell, you *were* her daughter. And you're mine too."

Ingrid could only nod. She wiped away tears. "I feel that way too, that you were . . . are . . . my parents. I guess I was lucky to have four parents." Realizing that three of them were now gone filled her with a deep misery.

"I love you, Ingrid, but I can't live without Rachel. I want you to know that." Jay took her hand and squeezed with the barest pressure.

Her tears flowing faster now, Ingrid held on to her uncle tightly as if willing him the strength to go on. "I love you too. I want you here."

Jay shook his head. "I'm all used up. There's not enough of me left."

Ingrid put both hands around Uncle Jay's chilly fingers. The wretched thought came to her that because she hadn't been home in two years, she had forfeited her claim on her uncle's affection. What kind of a daughter did that? To a man as good and strong hearted as this one was? "I'm so sorry. I should've been here."

"You're here now. And I need your help."

"Anything, Uncle Jay, you know that. I can run the diner for a while, take care of you a little."

Jay had that frozen look again, his lips unmoving, his chin jutting out.

"Will you let me?" Ingrid frantically tried to think of what she could offer this person who had cared for her during that terrible time following her parents' deaths. Who had taught her she was cherished and wanted even though her world had shattered. For a month he walked her to school in the mornings because she was afraid to go by herself. It didn't feel safe to leave home, to do anything.

Uncle Jay moved his head very slightly. Was that a yes or a no? His knotty forearms strained as he pushed himself up. "I'm going to drive home now. I want you to wait an hour and a half and then I want you to come to the house."

The dogged note in his voice frightened Rachel. "Let me take you. I don't think you're in any condition to drive. I think you'd better—"

He held up his hand. "Wait here. An hour and a half."

"I'm not letting you go home alone."

Uncle Jay's voice was soft, almost tender. "There are some things that aren't your choice. Things you have to accept. That's a lesson that we all have to learn."

"Uncle Jay." Ingrid was pleading now. "I need you."

He nodded, pursed his lips. Then his face cleared. "And I need you to leave me my dignity. That's important to me now."

She thought he was about to add, *That's all I have.* But of course he wouldn't say that, not to her.

Uncle Jay walked, slow but straight, to the back room that had a door leading to a small parking area. He called out without turning, "And please put the *Closed* sign on the door."

Ingrid stared at the clock, at the hands registering 10:45, and wondered what more she could have said to change his mind. Uncle Jay wanted out of this world and there was nothing she could do about it. Her hands tingled and nausea gripped her stomach. She got up and listened at the curtain to the back room. She heard a car start. The sound vibrated inside of her.

Retracing her steps through the diner, she went to the front door and slipped the *Closed* sign into a corner of the window. She shut the overhead lights off.

Behind the counter she paced back and forth, making sure the grill was off and the toaster unplugged. The refrigerator hummed.

Her mind seemed to freeze as she stood with her back to the counter. Her legs went wobbly. Just when she thought she couldn't bear another second, a thought broke through: *Closed doesn't mean finished.*

Ingrid bolted through the room, through the curtains into the back and out the rear door. The sun dazzled her eyes. She blinked to see her uncle's car, a blue Camry, waiting in the parking lot near the entrance of the street, idling. She ran to the passenger door and opened it. Uncle Jay's head rested on the steering wheel.

All Ingrid could think of was that her uncle had taught her to drive, patiently coaching her on those long afternoons when they headed out into the country on rough gravel roads. She often got lost, but he always knew which way to turn and which way to go toward home. "Uncle Jay?"

He didn't say anything, but Ingrid could see his back rise and fall as he breathed. He had gotten so thin.

He turned his face toward Ingrid. When he saw her, he looked the way she had often felt on those long walks to school, like he had been scared but now was relieved.

"I knew you'd come," he said.

Pueblo Luna

Pueblo Luna. *Pueblo Luna.* I dream of a bare street in the dusk, twilight meeting the tops of the mountains, light dipping and dropping until the peaks are swathed in dark purple. My shoes make hollow clicks on the street; there are no sidewalks. The heavy oak front doors face the street, always closed, the windows always shaded. Does anyone live inside any one of them?

Dream by dream, I visit all of those houses: creeping up the curving walks, looking for a crack of light, straining for a dog's low growl, the bicker of two people arguing over who had not paid the electric bill. I raise my hand to knock at each door, but each time let it fall, keeping the silence. Six houses, six front doors, maybe eighteen windows in all. The pueblo-style houses hunch on the street like shadows, unlit from within and looming from without.

~

I was a girl of ten when the dream bloomed night after night. The street stood for secrets, possibilities. Anything could happen behind those heavy wood doors. I would wake, ears sharpened to the sound of coyotes outside, keening far away in the distance. The floorboards in the hall outside my room creaked. My heart sang in my ears. Something waited, out of reach. Remember what it was like to run as fast as you could, your legs churning harder and harder until you were sure that if you jumped off a curb you'd take off and fly? Away from everything you knew.

By the time I was thirty I had lived away from New Mexico for thirteen years. I had forgotten the old dream. I met Diane and my heart raced when I was awake. Then a different dream troubled my nights: she and I waited for a train in an unknown country, another mountain town, sprawled in a valley facing soaring rock.

But when the train stopped, Diane got on and held up her hand. "Not now." The dark smooth curve of her hair obscured her face.

"You can't leave me here." I looked around the station in a panic. The people standing there had eyes as blank as those on the faces of sculptures, eyes that reflected nothing, recognized nothing. Where were we and how would I find my way home?

Diane smiled a sad, tender smile. "In time," she said.

During the three years we were together, daily living was forever changed, the world remade by our union. I would come home and if she hadn't yet arrived, I had the sense of life suspended, time hesitating until she returned, then the seconds gathering once again.

When I was thirty-three, Diane died. A sudden onset of esophageal cancer, a few weeks of medical terror, and she was gone. I was left alone, waiting as I had at the station, not knowing how to go forward, having forgotten how to go back. If losing her had a sound, it was of doors slamming, one after another, along a long line. No matter how fast I raced toward each open door, it clanged shut before I reached it.

I moved back to Albuquerque after I lost Diane. The streets around the new house I rented seemed peculiar to me. This strangeness was healing, because I hoped that if everything—the colors and shapes of the houses, the plants twisting along fences and walls, the intersections of streets—seemed different, I might miss the past less.

It didn't work. It's possible to live life by halves, but not to thrive. Something is always missing.

And then one day I began to explore the neighborhood where I lived. I learned the area one street at a time. I found a coffee shop on a broad avenue flanked by trees. Next to it was a bookstore that hired me to handle orders. When I wasn't working in the bookstore, I sat in the coffee shop, making up the stories of the other regulars, many of whom appeared to be writing stories of their own.

One day I strolled along N. Fourth Street and there it was: a street sign that said *Pueblo Luna*. At first I skirted the narrow avenue, reluctant to explore the quiet lane that invited speculation, to see if there really were six houses seemingly isolated from life.

And that's when the dream returned, the one I had had as a girl about the street with the clear view of the Sandia Mountains. This time I approached the first house, chocolate-brown stucco with tall windows and cracked wooden headers over each window. The stucco peeled off around the crown of the building. In front of me was the closed front door with no window. I raised my hand to knock, and my knuckles made a dull thump as if the wood absorbed rather than amplified sound. No one came. In the center of the door was a metal knocker, rusty and heavy. I raised it and dropped it three times against the door. After this second knocking, I heard feet shuffling along the tile floor, closer, closer.

An old woman with hair wrapped in tight strands around her head opened the door. Only about five feet tall, she stared up at me with wide dark eyes. "You." She stepped aside, gesturing for me to come inside.

I waited, looking down the street to see if anyone else ventured out into the front yards or onto the street. Only the dust blew in a sudden gusting wind. I stepped into a foyer that was crowded with pottery and baskets. Squat, blue-glazed clay pots anchored each side of a small and narrow table. To my right was a hallway. Empty. Another echoing hallway led to the left. Warm-toned Saltillo tile stretched as far as I could see.

"Come," the woman said from somewhere down the end of the right hallway. Her voice sounded just above a whisper, like grains of sand sifting when you pour it from one hand to the other. I wondered how much time I had until all of the sand would slip through her fingers.

I followed her into a room with a large bed and a thin metal lamp that curved around the headboard. A wardrobe painted turquoise, red, and tan stood across from the bed. Tall windows covered one wall and faced into the backyard. An elliptical flagstone patio surrounded by roses and purple blooming penstemon rested in the cool morning shade.

The room was a replica of the one Diane and I had shared. At the window, I placed my hands on the glass, aching to see Diane's willowy limbs swaying as she tended the plants.

I turned to see the woman staring into the yard with an abstracted air. A small smile lit her eyes. "Is it as you remember?" she asked.

Nodding, I turned back to the yard. I willed Diane to give me a sign. Without her, the room and the world outside were only stage settings. "Where are you?" I asked, my voice hoarse, unused. Our love, like the past, had little use for words.

Behind me, a door closed. The woman had vanished, but instead of panic, a wave of hope swept through me because her leaving made the room complete. This place couldn't be home, couldn't contain the spirit of Diane with a stranger here. I didn't try the door to see if it was locked. I wouldn't be leaving anytime soon.

The patio door swung open when I pushed on the latch. I stepped out. The air smelled of honeysuckle and high dry air. My lungs expanded. Had I taken a deep breath in the year since Diane had died?

Outside, bees flitted from one coral honeysuckle flower to another, buzzed on the purple Russian sages. A white-breasted nuthatch crawled headfirst down the ponderosa pine. In a low-walled enclosure, a round pond winked under a cerulean sky. Diane had built the pond herself and stocked it with koi. The water rippled in time to the low gurgle of the pump. I peered into the pond; the outline of my face wavered back at me. A small fin flipped below. Life was still here.

Patio furniture faced the pool. Choosing an upright metal chair, I sat very still. If someone looked out the bedroom window now, would they wonder if I were made of stone?

Yet I wasn't a statue, but rather a being attuned to Diane's approach. I waited. The light blazed at midheaven, then gradually lowered as the shadows lengthened into late afternoon. I was content to hold vigil, for Diane, for our life together.

At twilight, a figure entered the yard at the far gate, weaving along the path, wearing a tunic as blue as the sky. I rose, drawn as if by a piper's song. I began to run.

Our shadows melted together near the pond. As we joined, each said to the other: *You came home.*

Words Shimmer

Gertrude Stein is writing her life. In her studio in the hours before dawn, her pen fills page after page. She has dreamed of this room—the most remarkable room in the new century—all her life. Here, time past and time future flow into the continuous present. Every detail begs to be recorded.

But Gertrude does not write of the atelier at 27 rue de Fleurus. She writes about her parents and grandparents, of the strange alchemy of land and family and psyche. She will call this book *The Americans* or maybe—she draws a line through the title on the first page of her stack of pages—*The Making of Americans*. Even though she does not write of it, this room inspires her; it gives her courage.

Each Saturday evening, the room fills with guests. Gertrude cannot predict who will come on any given week. In a way it does not matter; regardless of its occupants, the protocol of the room is the same.

One man talks on these nights. The outpouring of his verbiage astonishes. His hair bristles with energy, strands coiling like wire around his head. A film of sweat slicks the long face. His round spectacles glow as his mind, bewitched, roams freely.

He is Leo Stein, Gertrude's older brother, and by his own admission, a genius. He talks—incessantly, urgently—about art. He navigates a sea of paintings: Cézanne's apples, entombed and lovely, Matisse's reclining nudes, Renoir's striking heads, Picasso's girl with the ugly feet. Canvases pack every wall. Stacked one upon another in a cacophony of color and line, the pictures hold court in silence. They articulate a language all their own.

But Gertrude hears only Leo. His muscular voice rises and falls, cascading into the ears and mouths before him: "What is true of art is true of genius . . ." His long frame sways under the weight of his genius, arms pointing to a swirl of blue, a smudge of ochre. "Cézanne did two things—he emphasized color and he simplified forms."

Gertrude observes the people who come and go. She notes how they speak; she watches how they listen. A flicker of an eye, a favorite phrase—she records their habits.

Too many words pour from Leo's mouth to digest, but the flow of his speech intrigues her. With one ear she captures phrases falling out of the sky of his knowledge: ". . . the pure contemplation of values . . . to appreciate one must apprehend . . ." With the other ear, and both eyes, she monitors the atelier. Bodies—eating, drinking, swearing, sweating, and most of all, talking—fill the room. A circle of men crowd Leo.

"You're wrong! Matisse is not truly *moderne*. But Cézanne . . ."

"That isn't art. That's just doodling."

"It's propaganda."

"Art is alive."

"Realism is dead. A stinking corpse."

"Cubism . . . so ugly!"

"Not ugly, modern."

"Art should mean something."

"The fetishism of art is absurd."

The men punch the air with their fists, their cravats flying in swirls of red and yellow and blue, like tiny kites taking off and crashing. *Bad sailing, bad sailing,* Gertrude thinks idly, taking phrases she hears and combining them in ways that interest her: *Ma-tisse, tease, teas, tea-licious, delicious* . . .

Gertrude occupies her own throne in the room, a large brown chair near one wall. She sits in her coarse corduroy clothes, also brown, hands planted on knees. The chair anchors her in the ebb and flow of the room's current.

She has watched this room invent itself since 1903. Quiet in the early years, she begins now to find her voice. A big woman, comfortable with her flesh, she laughs long and often. People often remark on her laugh, erupting from deep in the belly, rumbling, dancing, bursting, and on her voice, marvelously warm and sure. A group of young men surrounds Gertrude. They nod and applaud. Mostly they listen, their faces raised like baby birds waiting to be fed.

A visitor to the salon might observe how the world is split asunder by these two, brother and sister, the lean male spewing forth his passion, the stout female spilling over with mirth. Both talk chiefly to men. The women, where are they? If one scans the room, overlooking the clamor and the laughter, one finds a calm corner. There, a dark-haired, thin woman applies a fine needle to a skein of fabric. The skin of her upper lip glistens, her long neck arcs over her needlework. Three women perch in front of her, murmuring. All wear splendid hats that shield their faces and mute their voices.

Gertrude learns that this petite creature, her clothing as vibrant and alive as the works of art on the walls, holds forth in her own way. Like the paintings, her silence speaks. She is a vital link between Leo, the brother with the arrogant voice, and Gertrude, the sister who laughs. The link has a name, simple and plain: Alice. People say that if you want to meet Gertrude, you have to ask Alice.

Gertrude and Alice met at Gertrude's brother Michael's house in Paris. They liked each other at once. Gertrude's voice, the brooch that she wore, and a mystical bell tolling of genius drew Alice, as Gertrude wrote later. Did Gertrude put words into Alice's mouth when she named the three in whom Alice saw genius—Gertrude Stein, Pablo Picasso, and Alfred North Whitehead? For to Alice herself at the time such markers meant little.

Alice divines Gertrude's remarkable presence. Gertrude senses Alice's quality of attention. The nuances of connection fascinate them both and draw them together—along with of course the more obvious things, like Gertrude's bold physicality and Alice's exotic beauty.

Alice quickly becomes absorbed into the world around the Steins; she takes French lessons from Fernande, Picasso's mistress, and comes to dinner at 27 rue de Fleurus. Soon Alice is there so often that she ceases to be a guest. Already she types Gertrude's manuscripts, assists with the running of the household, consults with Hélène, the cook. In short order, Alice is indispensable.

Sometimes the Picassos come to dine also, as do Madame and Monsieur Matisse or Max Jacob or Guillaume Apollinaire with Marie Laurencin or possibly Isadora and Raymond Duncan. If they come on a Saturday night, others join them after dinner, for it is then that people come to gawk at the paintings and to argue.

The Saturdays are always the same: Leo first outlines for his guests—he designates them his pupils—one or two theories about art. He tells them how to look at paintings, particularly these paintings on these walls. He touches his beard, adjusts his glasses; he points, he pronounces: "All vital appreciation has a certain simplicity."

Some listeners incline their heads in assent; others applaud Leo's erudition. Two or three voices join in. And then, with no warning, quarrels erupt: one man stops in the midst of nodding, his eyes filming over with confusion or mockery. "Oh, no," he says. "That is rubbish. All this," his hands sweep the room, "all of this is rubbish." Perhaps his arm halts at Matisse's *Woman with a Hat*, that lurid riot of Fauvism. Sometimes the man stalks out of the room. More often, other voices join in, speed up, and dispel their views in a hissing rush like the swirling water in a tidal pool. Then the arguments begin anew, only louder. The energy of the room spins into a vortex, gathering and dispersing, building and releasing.

Alice came to Paris in 1907 with a female friend, Harriet. She planned to stay for a month and then return to the States. Harriet enjoyed her visit but missed American food, American talk, American ways. Truth be told, she began to miss Alice. For she saw immediately that Alice had fallen in love with France, with Paris, and with Gertrude Stein.

Like so many, Alice chose to stay in Paris. She escorted Harriet to her train at the Gare du Nord and waved goodbye. Alice had found her destiny in the form of a city, but most of all, in the form of a person. She would say later that Gertrude found home with her language, with English, but that for her, home was always Gertrude.

Alice is an artist whose métier is people, and her particular canvas is Gertrude. She found her own family in San Francisco to be lacking. Perhaps her father, like Leo, dominated others. Whatever her history, she sees quickly that Leo is a bully and that his chief weapon is his voice.

Leo extols art, but he excludes his sister's writing from the realm of art. To him, Gertrude's writing does not signify. She, the younger sister, seems immune to Leo's scorn. Yet at times Alice notes Gertrude's half-closed eyes pointed toward her brother as he preaches, her mouth drawn into a heavy line. And Alice . . . Alice watches Gertrude watch Leo. The small head darts in his direction as his rising voice carries above that of his sister's. Instinctively, Alice makes a note every time Leo overshadows or neglects his sister. She keeps a balance sheet of slights in her mind, and she does not forget.

Unlike Leo, Alice believes in Gertrude's writing from the very beginning. Gertrude writes—simply, astonishingly—about the real business of living. For this reason alone, Alice knows that Gertrude's work will shine. Although they live in Paris, Alice believes that Gertrude's art will resonate with Americans. Americans flock to Paris, the harbinger of the future, the vortex of modernity. Above all, Americans worship the new.

One evening Alice meets a woman named Mabel Dodge, a friend of the Steins. Mabel, too, thinks something revolutionary exists in the atelier. Mabel says to her confidentially: "People come to the Steins for the fun of it. They look at the art. They listen to Leo. But they don't—they can't—take it in. They scoff as they leave. They don't realize that they are changed by what they have seen."

The pictures, so vivid, so strange, change Alice. Odd how the pictures never become quite familiar. Partly this is so because the frames on the wall change: Leo and Gertrude argue between themselves, they buy and they sell and they trade. The siblings consult Vollard and voilà, perhaps an older Cézanne exits the studio and another Matisse (he is still greatly in favor) enters.

Some paintings inhabit the room more fully than any human. They hold court, like the somber 1906 Picasso portrait of Gertrude's head, all tan and brown. The head, cubist and stark, dominates the wall above Gertrude's chair so that she may sit beneath it. The portrait doubles her presence in the room. The head on the wall never changes, unlike the living one: the essence of the real, the painting remains Gertrude, forever.

Alice notes the comings and goings, the fixtures and the ephemera, of the room. She photographs the details in her memory. She knows that nothing exists without an audience. Leo proclaims that art requires a champion. Fame of any kind requires the same. And both Gertrude and Leo crave *gloire* above all else.

Alice sits, her watchful eyes record. She listens and sometimes she speaks of what she sees. She is essential. Even the continuous present needs a witness if it is to become part of the celebrated past.

1913

Alice is aware of Leo's critical gaze. She sees him turn away when she comes into a room. He says less and less at the dinner table, in the salon. More and more he absents himself from the Saturday nights. When present, he duels with his sister openly, his voice rapier-sharp.

After three years, Alice's presence in the apartment alters the delicate balance of energy between the Steins. Gertrude's loyalties, bound to Leo for so long, shift. The strength of two now lies with Gertrude and Alice. Leo is left on the outside, still talking, but with no one listening.

Gertrude's *Three Lives* becomes a modest critical success. A year later her most abstract work to date, *Tender Buttons*, appears to the wonderment of a few and the puzzlement of many. Fame is not yet hers. But she has Alice, and she knows that if Alice sees her, she must exist. If Alice believes in her, she warrants belief.

Late one morning, Leo and Gertrude are alone at breakfast. Alice has ventured out for a special cut of beef for Gertrude's supper. Leo, always a fussy eater, one who chews his food endlessly, pushes his eggcup away listlessly.

"I hope you're protecting yourself," he says.

"What?" Gertrude turns her broad brow toward her brother. She sees how red-rimmed his eyes are, how thin and pinched his neck.

Leo lifts his hands impatiently. "When you make her your slave, she becomes your master."

"No one is a slave. Or a master. What do you mean?"

"Gertrude!" Leo drums his fingers on the table. In response, Gertrude slides her chair farther from the table, away from his pale flesh, from the nails that are too long and too ragged. Her brother continues: "Everything has a price. Total devotion has a price."

"Oh, yes," Gertrude says, "I know." She stares at Leo's thinning hair, at the pallid, shiny scalp peeking through. She has followed this man across the United States, across the seas, to Europe. Since birth, she has stayed close to him. All of these years, he never turned to see if she was behind him; he just expected her to be there. Even the sun needs the shadow of the moon.

Leo throws up his hands. "I don't want you to make a mistake. To misplace your trust."

Gertrude's eyes narrow until Leo disappears. The room still stands without him. "I don't think I will do that again," she says. "Do not worry. Especially you, you should not worry."

"I do worry," he says irritably. "Sometimes you are careless."

"Have you made a mistake?" she asks him.

"What do you mean?" Leo's eyes dart around the room.

"You must have," she says, almost dreamily. "You change your life so often." Gertrude thinks of her brother's many professions—biology, history, philosophy, art history, painting—all started with passion and halted with ennui, suits of clothes he put on with care but discarded with indifference.

"I? How can you say that? You who left your medical studies, two courses short of becoming a doctor!"

"You had already left several lives behind by then. You came here, to Paris. I came with you."

"Listen to me. You are like a mighty oak that is being strangled by a clinging vine. Alice is that vine. She will stifle you." He pauses, sputters: "What about your . . . your writing? She will smother that too."

Gertrude smiles. She is not fooled; she has heard Leo pronounce her writing gibberish to anyone who would listen. "She helps me write. She has a good eye. A sound ear."

Leo is silent. Against his inner eye, he sees the blank slate of his life. Gertrude cannot write, but she believes she can—thus, she is a writer. He sees the flaws in everything; how can he believe he is anything? His sister's ignorance is her shield. For a moment, he envies her. Then, he folds his napkin with elaborate care. "Don't say I didn't warn you."

"No, I would never say that." The open planes of Gertrude's face close against her brother. His tirade against Alice shows what a monster of egotism he is, how he would do or say anything to safeguard his own comfort. Gertrude intuits that she is simply a touchstone for him, a piece of furniture reassuring him that the room is still the same. It is possible that he wouldn't even recognize her unless he expected to see her.

And yet, her heart softens again: he is her brother. She feels deep inside an unformed desire, still strong. If she could name the desire, it would be that someday he might appreciate her.

Leo leaves the table. Gertrude goes to the atelier to study. She reads again the works of Henry James, the brother of her mentor, William. She wonders if William James admired Henry's writing. Or did he envy his younger brother, surely a genius, whom many called the Master? Perhaps all older brothers covet the talents of their younger siblings.

$\sim$

Several days later, Alice walks round and round the Luxembourg Gardens with Gertrude. She clutches Gertrude's arm as they sweep along the paths. Rough white pebbles crunch and crackle under her shoes. The walk glows with a profusion of plants and colors: the soft, tender masks of the pansies; the slender, waving stalks of lilies, stems bursting with orange and yellow.

Alice sees that Gertrude is distracted and she says impulsively: "I have a secret to tell you."

Gertrude slows and faces her, mouth amused and expectant. "Yes?" she says.

Alice leans over to tie her soft black boots, a curtain of purple dragging across her legs as she bends. Some think Alice looks like a gypsy with her capes and shawls, the long, looping earrings, her bright-colored scarves. Swaths of fabric cloak her thin frame. The veiling attracts Gertrude; it allows discovery as each layer falls away.

Alice straightens slowly: "Leo's love for you tortures him. He sees you turn away from him. He thinks you no longer love him."

Gertrude's face is dreamy. "I did love him. He was my beacon. I followed him to Harvard, to Johns Hopkins. When he left Baltimore, I went with him to London, and then to Paris. I was young. But now I am finding my own way."

"I'm not sure he wants you to find your own way." Alice's voice is beguiling.

"No. Leo always knows the right way for everyone. He would be the first to tell you so." Gertrude's laugh begins to rumble, deep in her belly.

"But this is serious," Alice says. Her lips brush Gertrude's ear: "He blames me. He thinks that I depend upon you too much, that I am like a weed in a garden, crowding out the plants."

"Nonsense. You are too magnificent to be a weed." Gertrude smiles at Alice's beautiful colors, sniffs her pungent perfume. "You are like this fruit growing in the garden. Luscious and ripe. He doesn't know you. It doesn't matter."

But Alice knows that Leo does matter. His rage explodes if he does not get his way. His anger is like the bitter poison of the snake when it strikes. Alice does not want her life, or her love, poisoned.

"Leo has failed as an artist," Gertrude says. "He cannot paint. At least, not well enough. That's what consumes him."

The word "consumes" alerts Alice, because Leo manages his world by consumption. She realizes that Leo regards Gertrude like one of his pictures, something to collect and to control. When he tires of her, he would like to take her down off the wall, sell her or trade her or put her in storage. But now that she has a will of her own, she has lost her currency. Yet Gertrude tugs at him. She is of his blood. More important, she is his audience. He blames Alice. He will never forgive her for eroding the bond that once tied Gertrude to him. Alice considers and comes to the conclusion that she doesn't care. She cares only about Gertrude.

She draws Gertrude closer. Such a strong grip, one that takes what it wants. "Leo envies your success." Alice studies Gertrude. And sees her lover's face express surprise, then cunning. Alice knows that it is hard for Gertrude to believe that she could surpass her brilliant older brother. But Alice also knows how deeply ambitious Gertrude is.

"Does he?" Gertrude smiles at the words *your success*, and in her eyes glitters the naked greed of a child.

"I think he will try to hurt you because people admire your work," Alice continues. "You must be prepared for that."

"Of course." Gertrude feels the shameful twist of betrayal in her belly, and then anger. She cannot tolerate the one who envies, the one who covets. Especially one who has had so much, the anointed male whom everyone assumed would conquer the world. Gertrude—a woman, a Jew, a homosexual—has had to make her own way. Of course, she has her fine mind, a good education, and a modest income. But talent and determination, these are hers alone.

Confused by her turbulent feelings, Gertrude muses: "What would make Leo happy? I wonder what he wants." At this moment she does not care what he wants.

Alice remembers Leo's straining, intense face as he cajoles his listeners, his penetrating will. Perhaps power is the elixir of Leo's happiness. "He wants what he wants," Alice says quietly, wrapping her shawl more firmly about her.

Shadows now darken the garden path. The two women continue to walk, their bodies close, close enough to feel each other's heat.

~

In the fall, after months of tension, Leo decides to move. The household, once joyous, falls into acrimony and suspicion. As Leo prepares to leave the rooms he found at 27 rue de Fleurus, he and Gertrude argue over the paintings. It's as if the paintings are the children they had together during the ten years they lived in Paris. Dividing them is wrenching, horrible, impossible.

The artist Picasso is a litmus test of Gertrude and Leo's division. When Gertrude brings home a cubist Picasso she has purchased, Leo denounces it: "It is a confusion, like all of his new work. It means nothing."

"It is a synthesis," Gertrude says. "Of Africa with his Spanish self. It is brilliant. And prescient."

"It is a confusion. Its composition doesn't work. It doesn't even hold the eye."

"You'll see: cubism is the new wave."

Leo smiles at her with pity. He is the connoisseur, she a mere amateur. Picasso's cubist works, like her writing, will never sell, never have a public.

Leo says nothing to Alice. Alice watches. She sees Gertrude struggle, sees her fingers running lightly over the frames of the paintings in mute farewell. Gertrude agrees: Leo takes the Renoirs, she takes the Picassos, and they split the Cézannes. To his sister's great pain, Leo insists on the Cézanne *Apples*. They divide the other drawings and paintings between them. Leo later trades much of what he originally takes for more Renoirs. Blank spaces are left on the walls and in the lives of these two people, twined together since Gertrude's birth in 1874.

Twenty-seven rue de Fleurus is at first quieter as the household settles. But then, the space left by the departed one closes over: the Saturday nights are again full of food and talk and paintings. Gertrude becomes the oracle of the new: "The creator of the new composition in the arts is an outlaw until he is a classic. . . . For a long time everybody refuses and then almost without a pause almost everybody accepts." Gertrude and Alice are like vines growing together around a single tree, and the tree is their life growing ever stronger, together.

Gertrude writes in her notebook: "In 1910, Alice moved permanently into the rue de Fleurus. In 1913, Leo moved permanently out."

1919

The Great War is over. Americans pour into Paris. Some never leave after they are discharged from the army. As Gertrude says: "The men are troubled and unhappy. They are a lost generation." Others also come. They come to write, to paint, to play music. Most of all, they come to experience the great moment that is Paris: it is the beginning of the new world.

And they come to 27 rue de Fleurus on Saturday nights. The paintings still dazzle. There are many new ones, stacked row upon row on the walls. Other things have changed: the salon has a new center. Opinions now flow from Gertrude's mouth: "Everybody who writes is interested in living inside themselves in order to tell what is inside themselves. That is why writers have to have two countries, the one where they really belong and the one in which they live really." The circle of young men around her grows and grows. She still listens and laughs under the Picasso portrait. But the uncertain woman who watched Leo explain is gone. In her place is the Sibyl of Montparnasse, who knows about art and life in the renaissance called Paris.

She has begun to call herself a genius. "And you, Pablo," she tells Picasso. "You are the genius of painting as I am the genius of literature." Picasso's reputation, like Gertrude's, continues to grow.

Picasso, annoyed by all this talk of genius—how can writing be compared to painting?—surveys the room. He notices, among others, the effeminate men, the masculine women: not men, not women, he thinks, but Americans.

In the kitchen, Alice sits with the wives, and with the women artists whom Gertrude doesn't talk to. Gertrude talks to some—Marie Laurencin, Mildred Aldrich, Natalie Barney, Edith Sitwell—but not to others. The kitchen is alive with delicious smells, of fresh bread, of fragrant soups. Alice, too, has found her place. The wives listen carefully, for Alice holds the key to negotiating the bohemian pathways of the city. More than ever before, if you want to meet Gertrude, you must ask Alice. If Alice disapproves of someone, that someone does not return.

Leo is still in Italy. Alice reflects on the wheel of fortune turning in its random path, favoring some, neglecting others. She sees that Leo Stein, arguably a genius, has somehow missed his moment. *Gloire* is not to be his. The finger of fame points, improbably, at his younger sister, once so awkward, so shy, and her female lover, a sorceress in Leo's view, a bewitcher of those stronger than herself. Leo has become "Gertrude Stein's brother." Leo, thinking Gertrude only his shadow, walked away from the rue de Fleurus. He left his shadow behind. Alice knows that a man who casts no shadow does not really exist.

Once so incendiary an intellect, so sure in his enthusiasms, Leo remains a cautionary tale. Of lost potential, lost horizons. Gertrude, the one planted solidly in the earth, keeps on writing, even when she lacks a public. Alice is her appreciator and her witness.

And now, after the Great War, as the world embraces the new, her work slowly gains traction. Gertrude Stein is a symbol of the new century. As she said herself, America created the twentieth century, and one American woman created the new literature in the twentieth century. Neither Stein was ever modest, but only Gertrude has accomplished what she set out to do.

Gertrude has made the rue de Fleurus her own, hers and Alice's. For now the atelier is even more a remarkable place. A space where the present moment is captured and repeated, through talk, through the wavering brush strokes on the walls, through the friendships that bloom there. Soon other literary geniuses will walk through its doors—mature talents like Sherwood Anderson, the young, beautiful, and hopeful like F. Scott Fitzgerald, Ernest Hemingway, and Djuna Barnes. The room cannot contain all of them, but like the light that beams through a Gothic cathedral and bathes its worshippers, it allows the essence of each to shine through.

Laughter rings in the atelier. Talk flourishes, but now the pronouncements are Gertrude's: "Remarks are not literature . . . life is tradition and human nature . . . when a new way had to be found, naturally we found Paris . . ."

Gertrude still wears brown, still sits under her Picasso portrait. The painting stays the same, and more and more her likeness to it grows. Picasso is not surprised at this. When he finished the portrait in 1906, their friends complained: "But Gertrude does not look like this painting!" "She will," he said.

Alice wonders about the words she spoke to Gertrude that day in the garden. What part did they play? She realizes how words can change the world. Once uttered, they root and sprout; they take on a life of their own. They sail into the world and collide with some things, merge with others. They make history.

Across the room, Gertrude's eyes find Alice. The two women share a secret smile. Both think, "She is my life." Talk surges around them, of life and art, war and peace. The room pulses with energy, levitates with living. Words shimmer like ripe fruit.

EXHIBIT B

Is It Really You?

"Is it really you?" The woman in a yellow tracksuit walked up next to Ellen at the bakery counter. The fragrance of the place was buttery, hints of cinnamon and apricot wafting about. Ellen was almost too hungry to pay much attention. She turned around. No one else was nearby—the woman had to be talking to her.

"Um." Ellen adjusted her glasses. Did she know this person? The woman had a hopeful expression. "I think you might be mistaking me for someone else," Ellen blurted out. Best to be honest.

The woman stuck out a stubby hand with very short fingernails. Gardener, Ellen thought. She could just see the woman grubbing about in the dirt. Probably everything she planted came up too. "I'm Grace Norris. You look just like an old friend of mine, Betty. Betty Vasquez. Haven't seen her since she moved." Her face looked hopeful again, the smile almost too wide, her teeth square and efficient-looking.

Ellen hesitated. Wouldn't the woman, this Grace Norris, have known if an old friend moved back to town? However, the corner bakery was a cozy, friendly place—the scones looked fantastic today (raspberry, her favorite)— so why not be cordial? "I'm Ellen Alger. I'm afraid I don't know Betty." She shook the woman's hand. It was warm and fleshy.

"Well, that's a shame." Grace erupted in a wobbly laugh. "I was almost going to say it's a shame that you're not Betty. But that's not your fault, is it?"

Ellen weighed in her mind the possibilities: the scones and this woman, or no scones . . . She sighed. "Do you live in this neighborhood?"

"Close by," Grace said.

The woman behind the counter handed Ellen her scone on a plate and a double latte. "Oh, thank you," Ellen said as she paid her. She smiled at Grace. "Nice meeting you." She selected a table by the window and took out a thick paperback. The essay she was working on was a hard slog. She had been looking forward to this break all morning.

She had just cracked open the book and taken one delicious bite when a voice above her said, "May I join you? You do look so like Betty. And I'm afraid my husband's out of town and I've been rattling around in the house all weekend."

Before Ellen could open her mouth, Grace sat down across from her. "I've managed to get out in the yard, cutting back the bulbs in the back, you know how dense the iris gets, but the rain today kind of put an end to that."

Ellen shut her book. It was a Patricia Highsmith. The mysterious British man in Tunisia had just pulled out his gun. "You garden?" she asked politely.

"Do I garden? Oh my, yes!" Grace's voice rose eagerly. "Do you like gardens? I don't mean to brag but I have one of the most spectacular English gardens around here. Profusions of flowers."

"Well, yes, of course, I do like gardens." Ellen heard her own voice with dismay. What was she saying?

Grace sipped her coffee, which looked to be mostly milk. "Then you must come and see mine! Really. It's only four blocks away, you know that really tall and narrow house at the end of Pine?"

Ellen licked a tiny morsel of raspberry from her lip. She felt cold all of a sudden. There was a house on Pine that had terrified her as a child. It was the kind of house that appeared in a Gothic tale, set way back from the street, a seeming apparition anchoring the nineteenth century in the present.

She looked at her watch. "I don't have a lot of time today," Ellen began, again wondering what she was doing leaving the door open to go anywhere with this . . . this *strange* stranger.

Grace waved her hand in the air. "Oh, no problem. It's a three-minute walk. I'd love to show you."

Grace was already on her feet, reaching for her coffee cup and draining it. She beamed down at Ellen. "I'd be honored for you to come over. Just for a minute."

Ellen nodded. She took a big swallow of her coffee and looked longingly at her plate. She had devoured most of her scone in a rash of nerves. There was something about this woman . . . maybe she had seen her before somewhere?

"Well, I can spare forty-five minutes," Ellen said. She had to put some kind of fence around this event. "I have a deadline today . . ." She sounded apologetic to her own ears; what on earth was wrong with her? This Grace

Norris arrived and turned a perfectly capable thirty-nine-year-old woman into a floundering nitwit.

Out on the street, a light rain had begun.

"I just happen to have this with me," Grace said, unfurling the largest umbrella Ellen had ever seen. It completely enveloped the two of them. "Bought this on my last trip to London. Can you imagine, silly me, traveling to Britain with no umbrella?"

Ellen thought frantically of a response. Should she tell Grace about her own trip to London? Should she compliment her on the umbrella? How ridiculous—it was a hideous blue and white affair. "I think the only time I was there it was sunny every day," she said in a feeble voice.

"Well, then, I hope you spent the good weather at Kew Gardens," Grace spoke briskly. "The world's greatest botanic garden. I could just live there. Sometimes when Roger is boring me to death, I think what if I just fly to London and volunteer at those gardens?"

Roger. Roger Norris, the name hit Ellen like getting coshed on the head by a crowbar. That was the man who'd lived in the spooky house on Pine when she was a kid. He was kind of a Boo Radley type, haunting the place. How old was Grace anyhow?

"Tell me this," Ellen said. "I remember that Roger's family used to own a house on Pine Street when I was growing up. Didn't they? Right at the top of that little rise . . ."

"That's the one," Grace said with excitement. "Maybe that's how I know you!"

"Well, that was thirty years ago or more . . ." Ellen began.

"Roger's family has owned it forever!" Grace leaned even closer toward Ellen, although the umbrella already made for close quarters around them. "He is, of course, some years older than I am."

Ellen frantically calculated how old Roger could be. She thought he was maybe forty-five when she was nine; that made him about seventy-five now. Grace didn't look a day over sixty. The Roger she was thinking of had always seemed old. But of course to a nine-year-old, everyone over twenty was ancient. Still. Ellen shivered as a fat raindrop hit the knee of her jeans and spread a chill along her entire leg.

Ellen walked with the woman down the street and onto Main. She remembered this street from when she had lived in this neighborhood growing up. Main Street had mom-and-pop shops that, if they were shoes, had aimed to be polished pumps but were now sadly worn down at the heels. A 1950s dowdiness prevailed, as if covered by a patina of dust that took even bright sunshine down a notch.

As soon as you turned off onto Pine Street, though, you entered another world. It was a tiny tributary leading to a dead end; reality seemed to vanish behind you.

Ellen thought longingly of the last bite of scone and the perfectly prepared latte she had left behind at the coffee shop, accompaniments to a long-awaited book. Why had she let this woman, Grace Norris, convince her that she had to see her garden? Ellen was not fond of gardens in general.

The street sloped upward and with each step the houses grew grander and older, their details sharp in the afternoon light—wraparound porches, mansard roofs, tiny cupolas perched like silos on the roofs, and front doors topped by fanlights framed in ornate stone. The houses were so large that they insulated the inhabitants from any activity on the street. Ellen remembered trying to trick-or-treat on this street with her brother. No one had answered the door. In fact, the lights had switched off at each house when they had knocked.

They were trudging up the slight hill on Pine Street now. And there, ahead of them, was the house. It was high and spiky looking, painted a kind of beigey olive green, sort of like army fatigues. The windows were long and narrow too, about the size of coffins she had always thought. How big was that anyway, like seven feet by three feet? Ellen slowed her steps. She looked at her watch. Only five minutes had passed. She felt like running away from this claustrophobic umbrella and crying "Help! Help!" Her legs felt heavy and exhausted, as if her coffee had been drugged. How could she run anywhere?

Still, she stepped away from the umbrella and turned to face Grace. "I'm afraid I'm not feeling very well," Ellen said. "I'd love to see your garden. Another day maybe."

Grace appeared not to hear her. "Here we are," she said cheerily.

Ellen took in the house's four stories. A fire escape ran up on the left side but only to the second story. From a third-story window, a white face stared down at her and then vanished. Had the person winked?

"Um, wasn't your husband famous for his roses? I seem to remember that from when I was a kid."

"Oh, goodness sakes yes. I used to say 'Roger, you don't have ten fingers but ten green thumbs.'" Grace beamed and Ellen managed a tiny smile. How could she get out of this? But she was curious about the face at the window.

"Who lives here now?" Ellen asked boldly.

"Well, you know Roger passed on—he was twenty years older than me—I was lucky I had him for all of these years. So it's just me now."

"I must have misunderstood. I thought you'd said earlier that he was out of town."

Grace looked stricken. "Did I? I'm still not used to him being gone. Sometimes I forget when I'm talking about him . . . I . . . ." She wiped a tear from her eyes.

"I'm so sorry." Ellen said hastily.

As Grace touched a tissue to her face, Ellen studied the third-floor window. Was Mrs. Norris keeping a hostage in the house? A grandchild who had been abandoned? Ellen seemed to remember the Norrises had two children: the son had died in one of those freak accidents on the playing field—his heart had just stopped—and the daughter was named something like Susan, Suzette, Sigrid. Did she dare ask about her?

They walked along a cracked brick walkway from the street and through a wrought-iron black gate that creaked as if it had never been used. The house glowered above them, a dowager without a sense of humor.

The drizzle had stopped, but the gloomy sky and the house cast a monochrome pall over Ellen. Yet in a few more steps they reached the back where a riot of color flooded the yard, almost knocking Ellen over with its brilliance. The garden seemed like a lost paradise, everything bigger and plumper and brighter than Ellen had seen before. Ellen wondered if the gray sky made the blooms pop, like a red rose against a neutral background.

She leaned forward to touch a begonia, flame-red with green leaves arcing away from the flowers. "Is it real?" Ellen asked.

Grace's laughter was high and light, all tears seemingly forgotten. "Of course. If you see it, it's real."

"Has this always been here?" Ellen took in the huge yard, segmented into wedges—each color had its own area, she realized—and arranged in a wheel around a tiered fountain, grand in the Roman way, with several streams spouting into the air. A plump sculpture of Cupid stood in its center.

The odd thing was that it was September and the nights were getting cool, downright cold. But here in the garden, the air felt fragrant and warm. A wrought-iron fence circled the area as if cordoning off the bounteous growth from the drab slabs of the house's walls. Ellen eased herself down onto a gray stone bench. From where she sat, she didn't see the gate they had gone through, only the fence. She wondered if it was possible to exit this place. But with honeybees buzzing, the fountain murmuring, the flowers seeming to flare open the more she looked at them, Ellen found that she didn't care.

"Ah, you're starting to relax I see," Grace said. "Time is very overrated as a concept, and certainly as a way to rule your life, I find."

Ellen felt stuporous in the heat—the temperature seemed to be increasing.

"Let me get you something cool to drink," Grace said and disappeared.

As soon as she left the enclosure—and oh, Ellen wished she had seen how Grace had maneuvered out of the garden—a child stepped out from behind the sculpture in the fountain.

"Were you looking at us from the window?" Ellen asked.

The child, with beautiful brown skin and intense hazel eyes, nodded.

"Do you live here?" Ellen noticed that the child's clothes were antique, a white broadcloth shirt tucked into velvet breeches and black shoes with buckles.

"Sometimes," the child said—a boy, Ellen decided even though the long curly hair and full lips seemed at odds with the clothes.

"Only sometimes?" Ellen, light-headed in the heat, felt a prickle of fear. The child put a hand on her shoulder; his fingers were cold and his touch delicious. The desire to stand up and leave the garden leeched out of her.

"Here you are!" Grace bustled out from the house and handed Ellen a glass of something brown. Tea?

At the sight of Grace, the child hid behind a bank of hollyhocks, their red and pink blooms waving over his head. Ellen had a moment's fear that the other woman would discover him. Grace, in fact, held her head up in the air, motionless, the way a dog might do, as if sensing a change in the air.

"So you live here alone?" Ellen asked nervously, sipping the liquid that tasted both minty and bitter.

Grace cocked her head, and as she did, her face transformed from its genial mask into something withered and sad. Ellen put the glass she had been drinking from on the ground and stood up.

"I have to go now," Ellen said, again seeing the garden gate they had come through, but very far away, like the opposite goal line on a football field. Along with the wooziness she had felt earlier came a fierce headache.

Grace smiled a sad smile. "But I'd like you to meet Roger. And, oh, my son is here today—Bertie."

"But Roger is gone you said. He passed away. Didn't he?"

Grace reached out her hand and Ellen took a step back. Behind Grace, the young boy shook his head vigorously from side to side. Unsaid words seemed to fall from him like sparks: *Caution! No! Get away!*

The pure elixir of loneliness washed over Ellen. She longed to fall on her knees. Tears filled her eyes and she turned to run toward the gate, which telescoped away from her and shrank to a tiny thing.

Ellen's head was very heavy. She struggled to raise it. She blinked away the tears. The smell of fresh bread wafted toward her. She sniffed and looked around. She sat at a small table, its tile top cool to the touch. On it was her book, which had fallen shut. Her coffee sat in front of her, the milk's foam flat and dispersed. Next to it was an empty plate, white, with a few flakes of pastry straying across its surface.

She checked her watch to find that only a half hour had passed. That time now felt infinitely precious and irreplaceable. She had come to the café because she hadn't been able to write. Something was waiting for her, she had hoped, just beyond the next line of type.

The brilliant red begonias filled her mind. Luscious, promiscuous in their redness. The garden hovered just out of view but at the edge of her mind's eye. Its richness. Its promise.

At the counter, a pleasant-looking woman turned to the person behind her: "Is it really you?"

Duluth

Jackie knew it was time to go. She had been saying that for years, hadn't she? She had taken a two-year position at the community college in Duluth ten years ago, and after six months realized it was time to move on. Duluth, spreading along the shores of Lake Superior, once appeared to cradle her in its upper midwestern sturdiness and safety. Soon this permanence over the long winters caged her in. Dreariness set in. She clung to sources of light and warmth. That's when she had met George—he taught communication, she taught English—and they seemed to be having a fine time. For a while. For quite a while.

One afternoon when she was in the kitchen oiling the butcher-block counters (she had meant to replace them with granite but she hadn't thought she would be staying long enough for that to be worthwhile), George came into their little kitchen and stood by the sink. She guessed it was to get her attention; she focused with intensity when she oiled the counters. They stained so easily. People—*George*—were always leaving water standing on them or spilling mustard or leaving greasy food about. It really was a trial. Her mother always told her to give up already on the counters, who cared, and wasn't worn, well-used wood more beautiful than an unmarred surface? George came into the kitchen and said, "What I really want to say is, it's fine with me if you want to move to San Diego, but I don't think I can go with you."

They had argued that morning. George had grown up on the shores of Lake Superior, some little town in some little inlet. He didn't mind the winters, which seemed to last something like eight months. Jackie grew up in Los Angeles. Snow was a foreign language to her. It struck her speechless.

"Let's move," she said in January, a particularly arctic, particularly locked-up month in Duluth. Or that's how her arms and legs and hands and feet felt. Imprisoned in some kind of perpetual snowsuit, a vault of cold and ice.

"I don't think we should move in the middle of the school year," George said reasonably. But he was usually reasonable about her desire to move, because she mentioned it about once a week or maybe only once a month and when he took the subject in stride like this it seemed to make things better for a while.

But this time their argument took a different tone, a detour. George didn't sound levelheaded, for one thing. He had lost that even tone that made everything seem okay. Everything he wore even looked different. Usually, he wore a well-pressed pair of khaki pants to work with a blue shirt and sometimes a red tie. This day, his khakis were rumpled as if he had taken them on and off and sat on them and put them on again.

"I don't want to leave Duluth," he announced doggedly as if she had been trying to talk him out of living there, which she wasn't. She had just said, "Let's move," in the same easy way she always said it.

"Do you love your job so much?" she asked.

"I don't know about that," he said.

"Well, then." She put down the bottle of oil that said Boos on it, something special her woodworking guy had told her to use. She folded the cloth, pretty gooey now, in fourths and then again into eighths, opened it up again and spread it on the counter. "Do you love something else?"

"Like how do you mean? Of course I love my family." George's parents lived only fifty miles from them in a winterized cottage; it was so remote it felt like three hundred miles away. His brother, Dave, lived in the southern part of the state. The four of them called each other once a week.

Tears sprang to Jackie's eyes. One fat drop rolled down her face and off her chin and onto the counter. It stood out like a clear orb of some kind— the Boos was doing its job, repelling water. It shook like a tiny morsel of jello and then rolled a bit.

"Like, are you in love with somebody else, George?"

George gave her a helpless look.

Did the look mean *yes*, or did it mean *no*? She stared down at his feet, at his worn black running shoes. He never wore those to work, and she wondered what he had been doing with the rumpled clothes and the wrong shoes and all.

"I just want to know, George. It's not just about my wanting to move, is it?"

"No," George said. "It really isn't. I guess there is someone, kind of."

"Kind of?"

"Yeah, kind of."

"Do I know her?"

George just shook his head. Then, when she continued to wait, he began in a low voice: "It's not what you think. I'm not having an affair."

Jackie felt some relief. But only a little, because George had changed, hadn't he? Someone or something had taken him away, at least away from her. "What is it then?"

"I feel at home in Duluth. I have roots here."

"Okay, I think I knew that." The Kleenex box was on the counter, in the corner, and she reached over and took one and wiped her eyes and her mucky fingers. Then she stuffed it in her pocket. She resisted the urge to pick up the cloth again and work on the counters some more.

"George, what do you want me to do?"

His voice came in an uncharacteristic rush. "When I said there was kind of someone, that isn't true. There are several someones."

Jackie felt herself stiffen but she didn't say anything. She hoped if she gave George enough space, he would let her in.

He blinked at her now, his eyes bright. "A few of the other teachers and I have been working for animal rescue some afternoons after school, you know that place by the old highway?" At her nod, he said, "Yeah, that one. Critter Care." His face fell into a lopsided smile when he said the words.

Jackie picked up the cloth from the counter and folded it up again and then threw it in the sink. "Oh, George, why didn't you tell me before? I've been imagining that you were getting farther and farther away from me. You haven't been talking very much about anything."

"I'm sorry," George said. He pulled a chair out from the kitchen table and eased into it.

He patted the chair next to him. After a few seconds, Jackie sat down. He reached over then and took one of her hands, the skin slippery from working on the counters.

Jackie nestled her hand into George's warm and calloused and solid one. She let the silence between them linger.

"I don't want to run away from here just to make a change," George said. "If you need change, Jackie, maybe you could just let it happen. Moving isn't the only way, even if that's what you've always done before. What is it you'd really like to do?" he asked, still holding her hand as if the weight of his grip alone was keeping her from flying out the door.

Jackie found it soothing just sitting with George, holding his hand, and listening to him talk. She opened her mouth to say so when he put a finger lightly on her lips.

"I know," he said. "I feel the same way."

Jackie relaxed back into her chair. George's shoes were scuffed with what looked like bark mulch and dust—probably from handling some of the dogs at Critter Care. A little bit of mess was just part of George. Just recognizing that comforted her, as did her next thought. A dog. They should get a dog.

Jackie leaned toward George. He slid his arm around her shoulders. She scooched her chair closer to him. "Do they have any older dogs right now up for adoption?"

"There's one that I've had my eye on," he said. "She has red hair that shines in the sun, and she's very quiet. She knows what she wants. And she wants to be loved." George squeezed his arm more tightly around her. "Just like you."

"And you too, George." Jackie kissed him below his left ear. "You too."

David's Harvest

The summer I turned thirteen, I found out that families are made of pieces that don't always fit together. My cousin Eddie attacked my older sister Kath right in front of me, and I couldn't find a way to stop him. You could never count either of them out—Eddie was mean and Kath was tough—but it still wasn't an even fight.

Eddie and I were stuck in a boiling-hot truck in late August. My cousin was eighteen, but in his own mind raced the high road toward thirty. That summer, he would stare at himself in the truck's side mirror, smooth his dark curly hair and say: "I can't wait to see North Dakota in the rearview mirror." Eddie bragged that he liked big cars and big women and liked them both to be fast and hard to handle.

We had been hauling grain for three weeks. Showers and overcast days had us plodding on long after we should have wrapped up the harvest. We were all tired and used up, sick of eating dust.

The sunlight had faded hours ago. Uncle Charlie and Dad manned twin green combines, their headlights bucking as they hit rocks or clumps of dirt under the rows of swathed grain. Our job that night was to wait in the field until our fathers' hoppers filled with wheat one last time. Then, we would drive over, take the load, and head for the grain bins in the farmyard. I doubted we would get the field finished—we still had thirty acres to go, and it smelled like rain.

Eddie handed me a can of Miller from the cooler on the floor to see if I was man enough to drink with him, so of course I took it from him and popped the top like I did it every day.

"Jesus. We're gonna be here all goddamn night." Eddie pushed his cap back on his dark hair. A stripe of white shone at the top of his forehead above his tan. The beer can dangled from his broad wrist like a trinket.

"Probably." The cold beer tasted like iron, but it flushed the dust out of my throat. It was hot, even though it was long past sunset. There was no breeze. The heavy air clung to our skin like a damp sheet. The mosquitoes were biting pretty regular, too.

"Damn," I opened the truck door to let in more air. "I'm sweating like crazy."

Eddie turned on the radio he kept on the seat. KFYR was playing his favorite band, the Doors. Sweat oozed from Eddie's forehead and dripped along his hairline. Finally, he took his shirt off, wiped his neck and face, and then tossed the shirt onto the vinyl seat. It landed with a wet smack.

"You're gonna get bit to hell." I didn't expect Eddie to pay the least bit of attention to me. At thirteen, I was about as important to Eddie as one of the mosquitoes he swatted. He liked me a little better, but not much.

"Yeah, ain't this great?" Eddie giggled. "It's rotten work, if you can get it. But the tunes are still fine." He leaned his head back, the muscles on his thick neck standing out as he drained his beer. Eddie was tune-deaf and tone-deaf. He only knew the words in the title, so just chimed in with "Light My Fire" whenever it came up in the song, his voice flat and cracking.

I cranked the radio up. "Real nice. It drowns out the mosquitoes."

"Right, bud." Eddie grinned, his teeth white and even in the low glow coming off the radio. The DJ switched albums—more old '60s stuff that Eddie ate up. I guess because his older brother, Charles, liked it. When the DJ switched bands and announced "Happy Together," my cousin growled "Fan-TAS-tic . . ."

I slouched in the seat, trying for Eddie's cool. I reached over and dialed down the sound. "Mosquitoes are one thing, but I draw the line at the Turtles."

Eddie coughed out a laugh. "Hey, that's good. Really good, Dave. You're getting funny in your old age." Nobody else in the family called me Dave. I didn't much like it.

He slid lower in the seat and lit a cigarette. "So, how's your foxy sister?"

"Kath?" I guessed he meant her—Jenny was four years younger than Kath and away at summer school.

"Who else? Hello in there. You've got teenage brain-fry, kid. Look around you. Your older sister is one hot babe."

Hot babe? Kath? Amazing. She had just gotten married and she was almost twenty-five years old. Out of sight and off-limits, just like my parents.

"When's she goin' back to the Cities?"

"Middle of September, I guess. She's done with school. Except for bar exams." I recited what I had heard Kath say to my parents. "I guess those are a hassle."

Eddie fidgeted and pounded the wheel to the music. "Yeah, for pea-brains—but she'll breeze through those. Like she does everything else." He laughed. "Kath has a hell of a temper. I'd like to see her tell it to the judge." He nodded approvingly. "She'll be one tough bitch." Eddie slowly licked his lips after he spoke, as if the word "bitch" was a tasty snack.

I squirmed. "Kath's not always that way."

"Hey, relax. I think she's okay. She has guts. She has brains. Like I said, one hot babe. Beats the boring broads around here." Eddie cracked open another Miller and then bolted straight up in the seat.

"Oh, shit!" Eddie spotted Dad waiting for us across the field. He ground the gears into first and stomped on the gas. The truck strained against its load, then jolted forward as it swerved across the deep ruts and bounced up a low rise where my father waited. The spout adjoining the hopper angled out stiffly away from his combine like a traffic cop's outstretched arm. Aiming for the hopper side, Eddie slammed on the brakes and sent me sprawling against the door handle.

"Hard landing," he said carelessly.

"Jesus, Eddie, pay attention."

On top of the combine, Dad eased the release lever forward. The wheat, white in the moonlight, streamed from the spout and formed a high peak in the center of the truck bed. Dad caught my eye, jerked a thumb at Eddie, whose dark head slumped over the truck's wheel. A small smile came across his tired, dirt-smeared face as I gave him the thumbs-down in return. Eddie was a fuckup. Some things didn't change.

Once the hopper was empty, the spout-arm swung back to hug the combine, and the machine shuddered and trudged on. "Drop me at the other truck." I climbed back in with Eddie. "I'll check on your dad. You better take this load in."

"Is Uncle Chris pissed at us?" Eddie gestured at the combine and chewed on his bottom lip. Then he reached over me to open the glove compartment, brought out a pint of Jim Beam, and took a swig. His lips looked red and wet against the bottle.

"He's okay. But—"

"Want some?" Eddie tilted the bottle toward me.

"No, thanks. Maybe you should slow down. It's late—"

"I'd say your business and mine are not the same at all, junior." Eddie's eyes were bloodshot in his sunburned face.

The blood rushed to my face. "Okay, it's your funeral." The night was long and getting longer with every drink Eddie took. "Let's just move it. Uncle Charlie's going to be full any minute."

Eddie gave me a surly glare. For a second, I thought he was going to hit me. But all he said was: "Sure, Dave, sure." The engine whined as the truck lurched across the field. Eddie wiped a sticky hand on his pants. "Christ. Everybody's in such a damn hurry."

"It's one o'clock. We're just plain tired."

"I suppose I'm fresh and ready to dance. Get real." He spun the wheels across the fresh stubble and ground to a halt in front of the other grain truck.

"I'll unload and be back in twenty," he said.

I opened the door to leave, and he gunned the truck forward even before my feet hit the ground. He stuck his arm out the window, raising a beer in salute as he skidded off.

I hauled myself into the waiting truck, so old its red paint was history. I learned to drive in this truck at nine. Back then I had had to stand and stomp on the clutch to shift gears. It was 1:10 by the time I drove over to where Uncle Charlie's machine plodded on by the tree line.

Charlie stopped and waved. He got out of the cab and stretched, his stocky body a solid block atop the combine. He shook his head at the clouds drifting in the moonlight. "One more load tonight." His voice was scratchy from a day's worth of dust and chaff. "No chance we'll finish anyway."

"You'll just drive in when you get full then?"

"Yeah, I'll tell Chris to do the same. We'll meet you at home."

"I'll go back and help unload."

"Eddie there now?" Charlie's body, an older, heavier version of Eddie's, bent toward me. "He doin' okay?"

Early in the spring, Eddie had driven up the wrong side of a hill, collided with a postal truck, and totaled Uncle Charlie's new Ford Ranger pickup. So far, Eddie's smashups had only broken machines, but I guessed Uncle Charlie was just waiting for any one of Eddie's nine lives to give out.

"Sure." I gave my uncle the answer he hoped for. Charlie nodded and withdrew. Inside the cab, he adjusted his cap, flexed his beefy arm, stomped on the clutch, and pulled a lever. Once the pickup rotors were aligned to pick up the rows of cut grain, the combine lumbered on, eating its way through the wheat swaths. I checked my watch again: 1:30.

I snaked the half mile back to the farmstead along the section roads, littered with rocks and potholes. When I came up the hill by the house, the clouds had cleared some and stars were out. The moon and the truck's headlights turned the end of the yard into a bright field. Five round steel bins hulked in a semicircle. A rectangular steel Quonset—big enough to house the harvesting equipment—squatted at one end. Eddie's blue Chevy pickup flared like neon in the glow of the lights. It was parked at an angle near the aluminum bins with a shotgun mounted in the rear of the cab.

Fifteen yards from the pickup, Eddie's truck was backed up to the auger at the center grain bin, its bed cocked back at a forty-five-degree angle. Grain poured out from a gate at the end of the angled truck into the open base of the auger. The churning blades gobbled kernels and funneled them into the open top of the steel bin.

As Eddie hopped out of the truck, he caught the heel of his boot on the running board. I could see his face scrunch up but couldn't hear him cursing over the roaring of the grain auger. Eddie lurched over to the back of the truck and bullied the gushing grain like he was possessed—his shovel shone blue in the arc of the mercury light mounted above the yard.

I parked my truck just ahead of Eddie's. He was edgy, and I just wanted to stay out of his way. I checked the yard to make sure the dogs weren't outside.

When I turned around to check Eddie's progress, I caught my fool of a cousin showboating. Eddie sat astride the long auger shaft as if it were a horse and shimmied backwards up the sharply angled tube. He waved his gimme cap high in the air like a cowboy tipping his Stetson at the crowd from the back of a bull. Eddie hated farming. He really wanted to be a gentleman rancher, or better yet, a cowboy riding high on the rodeo circuit. He grinned at me and raised the hat higher.

I hustled over to him, skidding in grass already wet with dew. "Eddie, get down!" But my words were swamped by the full throttling roar of the auger. Eddie couldn't hear a damn thing I was saying. Eddie balanced precariously only a few yards above the base of the auger, which gaped open like a greedy mouth. Coiled shafts of metal spiraled the grain up the chute; the thing snarled like an industrial-strength meat grinder.

Halfway up the auger barrel, Eddie reversed directions. He slid down the tube, his arms angling out to his sides like wings. My lips felt numb as

I tried to holler loud enough to be heard. The only safety covering over the base of the auger was a thin vertical strip of metal. There was plenty of room on either side of it to swallow a foot or a hand. As his boots and blue jeans headed for the auger's mouth, I imagined a familiar nightmare scenario: Eddie's shoelaces or the bottoms of his pants catching in the whirling blades and sucking him in. Every harvest season some hapless farmer lost an arm, a leg, or his life just that way.

But Eddie's shoelaces didn't catch. Instead of jumping to the ground, he stood now on the metal guard, balancing on a strip of steel three inches wide, nothing but his beer-and-bourbon sloshing equilibrium between his feet and the churning steel rotors. Arms crossed on his chest, he frowned at the thinning stream of grain feeding into the auger.

It was 1:45. Too early for Dad and Uncle Charlie to return. No matter how hard I waved at him, Eddie ignored me, so I ran for the house. I was through the gate and about halfway up the sidewalk when the door opened and Kath came out, wearing a faded blue shirt of Dad's that swallowed her thin frame. She looked focused and crisp, like she had been up and working all this time herself.

"Kath . . . " I fought to keep my voice steady.

"You guys calling it quits? I have some supper ready." She pushed long, straight brown hair out of her face. Her eyes noted the mute appeal in my face, and then studied the yard. The truck was angled at the bin so that she could see the auger and the truck in profile. Kath's body tensed as she caught sight of Eddie, his body teetering on the auger.

"What's he doing?" She didn't wait to hear but took off at a clip down the sidewalk. Then she broke into a hard run, arms pumping the air as her long legs carried her through the gate and into the outer yard where the trucks were parked. I ran behind her like a shadow.

Eddie still stood on the auger guard, weaving slightly, as if hypnotized by the spinning rotors. Before Eddie could even raise his head and focus, Kath rushed behind him and cut the auger's motor. Almost in a single motion she hurried to the truck, opened the door, reached in, and released the hydraulic lift. With a hiss, the truck bed slowly settled back into a horizontal position in line with the cab. Kath leaned against the now-closed door of the truck, her eyes on Eddie. Stunned by Eddie's close call, I squatted on the hard ground off to one side of the truck, unable to muster the muscle to move.

"Hey." Eddie jumped off the auger barrel. One shoelace dropped inside the now-motionless shaft, and harmlessly slipped out. But the auger blades, and the carnage that could have been, kept my attention.

Eddie was oblivious to his near escape. Guys like him never knew their own luck. They only complained endlessly when it ran out. And it always did.

Eddie's forehead knotted in a look of pure outrage. "God damn it, woman, what are you doing? Can't you see I'm working?"

I was so relieved that the crisis was over that when Eddie puffed up his chest and ranted at Kath, I wanted to hoot with laughter. He looked like a cartoon Ralph Kramden shouting at his wife. Kath didn't laugh. She stood up straight and took a step toward Eddie. "I can see that you're smashed. Go home, Eddie. Before you hurt yourself. David and I will finish this up."

Eddie's chin jutted toward her. "*Hurt myself*—Christ! I could do this in my sleep. This is my load. I'll finish it."

"You're finished already." Kath swept past Eddie. She squatted by the open auger base and folded the edges of the tarp over the machine's mouth. Eddie's glazed eyes followed her, seemingly fixated by her sure movements. She turned her back on him, headed for the truck, got in, and started the engine. The engine complained with a high whinny as she drove over to the big Quonset. I knew then that Kath was nervous—she had forgotten to shift out of first gear.

Eddie stood stiff-legged, hands tucked into his belt, watching her. When she stepped out of the truck and began to walk toward us, he expelled a gob of spit that splatted in the dirt near her shoes.

Kath stopped. She kicked loose earth over the spittle. "Good night, Eddie. Do you want David to drive you home?"

"Fuck you." Eddie ambled over to Kath and grabbed her right arm. "Give me those truck keys."

Kath edged away from him. Her fist tightened around the keys. "Give it up. Just go home, will you? Dad and Uncle Charlie will be here any minute. You don't want them to see you like this."

"Like what?" Eddie's big hand twisted Kath's arm upward and behind her. Teeth clenched, she fought to wrestle her arm out of Eddie's grip. His hand looked bloated encircling the pale flesh of her wrist.

"Eddie, this isn't funny." Kath arched her body away from Eddie's thick torso. Her voice was low but strong. "Let me go. I mean it. Right now."

Eddie smiled. His dirty, flushed face tilted, making his grin lopsided, not much of a grin at all. "You want me to let you go? Okay." He shoved Kath away from him and she fell down, hard, on her back. The blue shirt twisted tight around her torso, riding up above her belly. Eddie fell to his knees and straddled her, pinning her arms against the ground. "You remember when you used to do this to me?" he said. "I sure as hell do."

The fall knocked the wind out of Kath. After several tries, she gulped air and gasped: "That was child's play. Years ago. We're not children anymore. Get off me."

Eddie just stared at her. He lowered his head, swinging his neck to one side. "You don't like this? I never liked it much either." He boldly stared at her breasts. Shame burned in my belly.

Kath grunted and pushed against Eddie. "You prick." She spat the words in his face. Eddie looked surprised, and then he grinned again.

The fury and frustration in Kath's voice jolted me out of my frozen crouch and over to where Kath and Eddie struggled on the ground. "Eddie, for Christ's sake." I planted myself behind Eddie, grasped his right shoulder, and tugged for all I was worth. His flesh was meaty and slick with sweat, dense as a side of beef.

Eddie's head whipped around as if he had been stung by a wasp. But then, the anger went out of his eyes. He shrugged off my hands and heaved himself off Kath. His rib cage heaved up and down with each breath, and when he moved his big body pushed me aside like I was just thin air. His jeans rode low on his blocky hips so that each time his chest expanded, his hairy stomach strained against the waistband and spilled over.

Eddie ignored Kath, who scrambled up, brushed the dirt from her jeans and tugged down her shirttails. She rubbed her wrists and arms as if they were numb. Her face was pale and set, the planes of her face gleaming in the light.

Eddie turned to me, almost casually. His neck flared bright red, but his voice kept its usual swagger. "Forget about the truck. It's still early. I'll just go swath that last slough of flax," he said, as if the two of us were alone. "We might be able to finish tomorrow if I do that."

"What? Eddie, you're crazy. It's two o'clock. In the morning. Come on, let's just knock it off."

Eddie hitched his trousers up as if he had infinite time, as if Kath wasn't behind him fuming. He just looked at me, a goofy half smile plastered on his face.

Kath raised her voice, which sounded as chafed as her wrists. "Don't touch anything. I'm warning you. I want you out of this yard in thirty seconds—"

But Eddie had already disappeared inside the Quonset. His feet scuffed along the cement floor as he circled the farm equipment. The structure's metal walls vibrated as the swather engine fired. Eddie rode the machine out and up onto a rise at the edge of the yard, then shifted the engine into neutral. He paused for a moment like a general on a hilltop surveying the battlefield. At the front end of the swather, a reel of wooden paddles rotated at low speed. These paddles swept the grain against the sickle, which cut the stalks so that the grain would lie down in swaths. "Versatile" scrolled in big letters across the machine's red body. The slow sweep of the paddles reminded me of the Ferris wheel lazily circling at the county fair earlier in the summer. But Eddie was anything but entertaining. He sat atop his equipment like a tank commander. He sliced one arm across the air, warning me out of the way.

I scrambled backwards away from the left front wheel. By the time I turned around to look for Kath, she was planted in front of the swather with a shotgun. It was Eddie's own gun, a Browning semi-automatic. She had grabbed it from the cab of his Chevy. I couldn't help but notice what a nice piece that gun was. My mind scattered everywhere rather than focus on the facts—that my own sister was leveling a loaded rifle at Eddie, that our first cousin was out of his mind.

Eddie hauled himself out of the seat and leaped to the ground. He stood in front of the rotating reel. "That's my gun. Keep your dumbfuck hands off it."

"And that's our equipment. Not yours. As far as I'm concerned, you're stealing it. If you get back on that machine, I swear I'll shoot you."

Eddie crossed his arms, swayed slightly but stood his ground. He swore at Kath, his face flushed. Their shouting was muffled against the roaring engine; it drifted toward me in muted waves. Their bodies seemed far away.

Kath edged over to me, keeping the gun trained on Eddie. "Go and turn that damn thing off. Take the keys out," she ordered.

I scrambled up onto the high, hard seat and cut the power. Snatching the keys from the ignition, I bailed off the machine like it was a live thing that could bite. The paddles slowed, then stopped. I looked out toward the road. There was still no sign of Dad and Charlie. I squeezed my eyes shut and prayed for them to get home.

"Hey, Kath, aren't you going to shoot me?" Eddie burst out with a cocky giggle to show us that nothing fazed him—sure as hell not a woman holding a gun she probably couldn't shoot. The laugh was loud and jarring in the quiet night, his voice ricocheting off the sides of the grain bins.

I opened my eyes. Kath still stood there, her legs stiff and planted, the gun leveled at Eddie. She took a step toward him. He automatically took a step back. Kath flinched and reached for Eddie. For a second or two I didn't get it. Then my neck broke out in a prickly sweat—I'd forgotten to set the brake when I cut the motor, and Eddie hadn't either. I stared at the platform of the swather as if my mind could will the levers to rearrange themselves.

The night air was still and eerily quiet as the swather began to roll heavily toward Eddie. "Eddie!" Kath screamed.

But there was no time. The Versatile lumbered down the slope and smashed into my cousin. One paddle blade caught him behind one knee. His legs just folded. He collapsed, limp with shock, and fell onto his face, his body neatly sandwiched between two blades—they fed him into the sickle like he was a stand of ripe wheat. His neck was twisted at a painful angle. The swather didn't have much momentum, so Eddie's body brought it to a stop, his left shoulder pierced by the sickle blade. Eddie was lucky— the engine was off, or his flesh would have been cut to shreds.

Kath set the gun on the ground and rushed toward him. "Don't touch him!" Squatting next to Eddie, Kath examined the position of the body where it lay between two paddles.

"The blades have him. I just don't know how deep." Kath hung over Eddie, her breaths fast and shallow. "I think the fall hurt him more than anything."

When she stood up, she rocked slightly back on her heels. I wondered if her knees felt as rubbery as mine did.

Eddie groaned.

"Come on, David." Kath nodded at me, and we both threw our bodies behind the left wheel. Nothing budged at first. Finally, we rolled it back just enough so that his head and arms were clear.

Before she touched him, Kath said: "Eddie, can you feel your legs?"

He could move his legs, thank God. "Here, grab my wrist," she said, wrapping one arm around Eddie's torso and offering him the other.

I wedged my right shoulder under one of Eddie's armpits, reached across his back until I locked hands with Kath, and together we hauled him out. Eddie tried to pull himself free, but it was Kath who pulled us through.

When he was clear of the equipment, Eddie raised his head a bit, wincing as he extended his neck. His face was scratched, his forehead bleeding some from falling into the dirt. Blood soaked his shirt high up on his back where the sickle had bitten into him. "Jesus, my neck is killing me," he whined.

"David, quick. Call an ambulance."

I stared in wonder at Kath, at her flushed and sweating face, her lank hair streaking across her face. The shotgun lay in the grass like the dead thing it was unless somebody aimed it.

"Do it now!" she yelled.

I turned to run toward the house, but a shadow on the grass loomed toward me. Mother stood by Eddie's pickup, watching, clutching a blue chenille robe around her body. She might have been a ghost lurking in the moonlight. My arms impulsively reached toward her.

She took a step back, her lips barely moving to form the words: "Just go. Call the ambulance."

When I stumbled back out into the yard, things didn't look so bad. Eddie's gun was back in its rack in the pickup. Mom looked steadier as she layered old blankets from the well house over Eddie, while Kath sat cross-legged in the grass, holding his hand.

The muffled blare of engines heralded the approach of Charlie and Dad. As the green tops of the two combines emerged above the hill near the house, Kath turned to Mom, then me: "I don't think we need to mention how much Eddie was drinking tonight. Or . . . or the argument we had."

Her voice caught on the word "argument" and I wasn't sure she meant Eddie knocking her to the ground and bullying her or how she had held the shotgun on him.

"But how does this make any sense if the drinking doesn't come up," I protested. "What about the swather? Aren't they going to wonder how in hell—and why—it happened to be parked outside at two in the morning? And why it was in neutral without the brake on?" I appealed to Mother, but she wasn't looking at me. Her eyes shifted back and forth between Eddie and Kath, as if weighing something.

"How are they going to know things like that? It was an accident," Kath spoke firmly and flatly. "Nothing more, nothing less."

"But Eddie attacked you. And what about his gun?" Panic thinned my voice.

Kath patted Eddie's hand. "What about it? It's over. Look, David, say what you like. But I'm saying it was an accident."

Eddie was plenty scared, but by this time he knew he was going to make it. The muscles of his neck and shoulders spasmed some, but he was moving his arms and legs freely. "What's wrong with you people? I'm in terrible shape here, and you're sitting around bitching at each other!" His head lolled on the ground. "Jesus Christ," he groaned.

Mother looked at me, her lips firmly pressed together in her tired face. "What good does talking about it do now, David? Eddie's hurt. That's what we have to pay attention to."

Around three that morning, I sat drinking Coke at the kitchen table with Dad. The bulb above the table encased us in a tight circle of light. Uncle Charlie, Mom, and Kath had gone off in the ambulance with Eddie to the hospital.

Dad leaned back in his chair, one fist tightly gripping a glass of J&B. The skin over his knuckles looked transparent. "I know Eddie was drinking again," he began.

His voice sounded raw, filled with dust from the wheat chaff and the lateness of the night. "I'm not going to even ask you about it. Even Charlie's going to have to face up to the fact that his son needs some help. You can't trust him. But . . . " He turned his face toward me. He still had his cap on, and his eyes were hooded. "Are you okay? What about Kath?"

"Kath?"

"Yes." He set the glass of Scotch down on the table, his tall, big-boned frame slumping around the glass. He folded his large hands limply between his legs in a helpless gesture. He spoke in a low, flat tone of voice as if he were conserving his energy for a big effort: "David, I want you to tell me, did Eddie hurt Kath?"

I shook my head and said quickly: "Kath takes care of herself, you know that."

Dad reached out and put one hand on my shoulder. My bones felt small under the broad grip of his hand. He squeezed the flesh gently. "Look, I know there wasn't much you could do. Eddie's over two hundred pounds. You're what—one-twenty?" His hand dropped away. "You're still a boy."

He drew in a deep breath, then let it out slowly. "I know Kath's tough. But it's not that easy for a woman. Eddie's a bear of a man. And he's a brawler when he drinks." He extended his hand again, the fingers grazing my arm. "You didn't answer my question."

The whirling metal rods in the auger and the sight of Eddie's shoelaces dangling above them still flared in my mind. "I think he might have wanted to hurt her," I said slowly. "But he didn't. Not really."

I winced, thinking of Eddie's big sweating body on top of Kath, the way he ogled her breasts and hips, his head swaying side to side like a shaggy dog. My stomach turned over and an acidy taste came into my mouth. I drained the Coke to wash it down. I wished I could wash away the night as well.

"Not really? I swear, David, there are some things you don't keep quiet about."

"No, it wasn't like that." I put my hands over my face. They looked like someone else's hands. Filthy and swollen, they were streaked with dried blood from lifting Eddie clear of the swather blades. "I'd die first before I'd let him do anything bad to Kath."

He nodded, waited for me to say more.

I spoke in a rush: "Dad, Eddie was fooling around on the auger. I think Kath saved his life."

He raised his glass and slammed it on the table. "Christ. I can imagine how he thanked her for that." He pushed away from the table and stood with his hands in his back pockets. He leaned his forehead on the glass of the big kitchen window, stared into the garden.

I didn't think he could see anything, shapes shaking in the wind maybe, shadows. I felt full of shadows myself. The night replayed in my mind over and over in slow motion: the lazy turn of the paddles, Eddie's body fed like fodder into the wheel, his face crunched against the ground. I pressed my fingers against my eyelids.

"That's fine, David."

"What?" I was startled to hear his voice, so low, like a sigh.

He turned away from the window. "You don't have to tell me if you don't want to. I'll talk to him about it myself."

"What about Uncle Charlie?"

Dad shook his head. The gray strands flowing back from the crown of his head pierced my heart. They looked so fine. "Charlie's made some mistakes himself. He won't be too hard on Eddie. Not hard enough."

"But if he thinks Kath—?"

"If Kath what?"

I recoiled at his sharp voice. "If he thinks Eddie might have hurt Kath. Or if she saw him do something."

My father smiled sadly. "Charlie doesn't hold women to be worth very much."

"I don't understand—he and Mom are great friends."

"She's the exception that proves the rule. Ask Kath—she knows what I'm talking about."

Ask Kath? I knew that she thought a lot of men around Devils Lake bullied women and treated them rudely. And when there was alcohol involved, behavior escalated beyond rudeness. But was Dad saying that Uncle Charlie—his own brother—was the kind of man who didn't care how women were treated? That he had a drinking problem and so no wonder Eddie had one? I wondered about Aunt Shirley and my cousin Leslie. Had they confided in Dad? Kath might know their secrets but she would take my head off if I even brought the subject up.

My father switched off the light over the table. "We better try and get some sleep."

"Dad?"

"Yes, David?"

"I don't know what to think. About tonight." I walked over to him and stood very close. I was aware of the heat from his body an inch or two away.

He hesitated. Then he stepped closer, so that our shoulders were lightly touching. "I don't know everything yet," he said quietly. "I can't help you." And then he turned and walked out of the room.

I never knew "everything" about that night. Eddie, with his usual luck, got off with a moderate injury to his neck—the force of his fall caused the damage, not the paddle blades or the sickle. The cut in his shoulder required only five stitches. He had to wear a neck brace. He whined about that all the time. He did some time in physical therapy and even managed to lose a few pounds before he was done. Except for a stiff neck, he was pretty much himself after two months.

Kath kept quiet about the whole thing. It wasn't like I wanted to talk to her about it, either. We were both embarrassed. Embarrassed to admit that we were scared of Eddie and didn't know how to deal with him that morning. We each had seen things we would rather forget.

Mother was furious with both of us. We found that out a day later when the three of us were working together in the garden, clearing out the last of the corn.

"If you saw that he was drinking, you should have told him to leave right then," she said fiercely. "I mean right now. Alcohol and harvest don't mix, and you both know it."

I felt guilty about the one beer I had drunk in the cab with Eddie. I wondered if she knew about that.

Kath was quiet, carefully stripping the graying yellow sheaf from a cob. Then, spotting the mealy brown track of a corn borer, she dumped the corn on the ground. "Mother, that's easy to say. But Eddie's not easy to get rid of. How would you have gotten rid of him?" Her lips stretched into a funny tense smile. "Outside of shooting him, that is."

Mother ignored the question, exploded instead: "My God, Kath, you're out of line!" The lines around her eyes and mouth deepened into a mask of anger. "That's a fine thing to teach your brother."

"Fine. But you haven't answered my question. Just how would you have conveniently removed Eddie from our yard? I'm a grown woman. And married. If you know a way to handle a situation like this, please tell me." Kath moodily plucked corn silk, sticky as a spider's web, from her fingers.

I knew Mother didn't think much of Kath's husband, Henry. She ripped an ear from a drooping stalk, its leaves already tinged with black, a sign the first frost couldn't be far away. With a practiced motion, she peeled back the tough covering, checked that the color was the right shade of yellow— she liked it really bright and ripe—and tossed it into the bucket at her feet.

Kath just stared at her, waiting. Mother fidgeted with the neckline of her blouse. "Eddie's not a responsible person. You are."

I tried to keep my head down and my hands occupied quietly in the corn patch—not easy when you're snapping ears off the stalks. I fumbled a lot because I was so distracted by what they were saying I could barely tell a corn tassel from a clod of earth. They appeared to be talking in some kind of code. I wished that my sister Jenny had been home and listening to this with me so that later she could explain what it all meant. Mother sure wasn't answering Kath's question. I didn't get how being responsible had anything to do with handling our rowdy cousin.

A blotchy patch of color brightened the pale skin of Kath's throat. "I'm very responsible, Mother. We both know that. But that doesn't change the fact that I was faced with a drunk. A stuporous gorilla who didn't listen to a word I said!"

Kath planted herself directly in front of Mother, knees locked, elbows out. Loose strands of fine brown hair strayed out of her ponytail into her eyes. She brushed them away as if they were pesky flies. "I really want to know—what would you have done?"

Mother's fierce tone evaporated. She sounded almost prim. "I'm sure you've managed situations like this with boys at parties—when they're drunk and not thinking clearly. You have to be in charge, so no one gets hurt."

She looked almost tenderly at Kath: "In a way, you have to save men from themselves."

"Oh great." Kath exhaled noisily. "Just great. So then who's left to save me?"

Mother glanced uneasily in my direction and then at Kath. She crossed her arms and hugged her chest. The skin puckered around her mouth. "I didn't say it was easy, dear. But it's all part of handling men. You know."

Her voice dropped, and I thought I heard a note of helplessness in it. "A woman just knows how to do such things. Before things get out of hand."

Kath took a clumsy step backwards. As if Mother's words had plugged her into an electric socket, she thrust her arms out wide. She thrashed against the stiff stalks, fighting to claim her space. "Oh, really, Mother, and what kind of woman do you have to be to know these secrets? And why the bloody hell didn't you teach them to your eldest daughter?"

Kath crashed through the rows and made her way through the grove north of the house. Her back looked as stiff as the blocky combines when they slogged across the fields, gobbling the grain and spitting out the straw. I watched the proud line of her shoulders until she disappeared into the trees.

Mother stood like a statue amid the corn, the stalks standing sentinel behind her, eyes planted on Kath's retreating body. Mechanically, she reached out and grasped another ear of corn. I heard a solid "thunk" as it landed in the bucket.

After a minute she looked up at the sky, at a huge cumulus cloud shrouding the sun. "I think it's going to rain," she said with a faint smile.

I didn't say anything, imagining Kath running as fast and as far as her frustration could carry her. Kath's anger seemed the right response to everything that had happened. Her anger had saved her from Eddie. That and her courage, which saved us all.

Coincidence

Bradley liked to know what would happen next. Always. He knew the alarm would go off at 6:45 (he always woke up fifteen minutes early so he wouldn't be surprised, but would he wake up if he didn't have that alarm set?); he prepared the coffee pot the night before and set the timer so the coffee would be ready at 7:01; the multigrain bread he toasted was always from the same bakery. He collected his newspaper after he hit the toaster oven button but before he poured the coffee. More of the same continued throughout the day. However, on this particular Monday, when he opened his front door and looked toward the driveway, he saw that all four of the tires on his car were flat. Wow, he thought, and tried to remember the last time something so completely unexpected had happened.

He walked out and sat down on his front stoop. Maybe the last time he had been this surprised was when Melissa left? She had turned on the toaster oven on his multigrain bread just as he came into the kitchen, hair plastered to his head from the shower, and said: "Bye, Brad. Oh, I like the sound of that. Bye, Brad, bye-bye."

That was two years ago, in April. He glanced at his watch. Today was April 16. The same day that she left.

He stared at the flat tires, but no matter how long he looked, not one of them inflated. Bradley guessed his baby blues had lost their power. Melissa had called attention to them back in the day. "You have the most fantastic baby-blue eyes," she would tell him, each time saying it as if for the first time. He and Melissa had gone to junior high together. Brad was now thirty-three.

"Shit," he said, but before very long he started to smile. He called work and told his boss he was sick. "It's like I can't move—no wheels are turning, you know what I mean?"

His boss said she knew. But he didn't think she did, not quite. The warmth in her voice almost tripped him into guilt when she added: "We'll cover for you, don't worry." He decided this day he would take her advice—he wouldn't worry.

Instead of heading for work at 7:45, Bradley checked his briefcase inside the screen door and headed for the park a few blocks from his house. He couldn't remember the last time he had gone there. It was springtime in Albuquerque. A few leaves sprouting, a lot of sunshine, and a bottomless blue sky. He took a deep breath—gotta love that high, dry air.

The park in his neighborhood was empty except for one woman on a bench feeding the birds. Long dark hair, parted in the middle, slim waist, broad shoulders under her long red shirt, long legs stretching to tomorrow. She was a knockout.

It was Melissa.

Bradley stood behind a broad cottonwood tree and watched her. She had a bronze carryall like a camera bag next to her on the bench. Melissa dipped her slender fingers in the bag and tossed out some coarse bits. Sunflower seeds? Bread crusts? Sparrows and doves clustered around her. Bradley felt like he was in a new version of *Mary Poppins*.

"I see you lurking behind that tree," Melissa said without turning her head.

"Do you live near here?" Bradley asked. What do you say to someone you haven't talked to in two years, someone you used to know so well you didn't have to say words aloud at all for her to know what you were thinking? Bradley wondered if all that secret knowledge had faded away.

Melissa looked at him then. "Remember that Ionesco play about the man and the woman who wonder where they've met before?" Bradley shook his head. Melissa tossed out a few more seeds. "The old couple are on the train, and they ask each other where they're from, which street they live on, what is their house number, and so forth. Each time they exclaim: 'How curious, how bizarre, and what a coincidence! It is perhaps there that we've met.' At the end they find out they share the same bed."

Bradley didn't know what to say. He didn't even know where to start, so he just waited.

Melissa finally returned to his question about where she lived. "About the park. Yeah, I just live on the other side—the far side, if you're in your house, the near side if you're in mine."

Bradley felt his mouth open and close, like a guppy trolling for oxygen. "You're kidding," he said.

"How curious! How bizarre! And what a coincidence!" Melissa quoted again to him.

Bradley slid out from behind the tree and slouched over to the bench. She pointed at the spot next to her. "Sit. Aren't you usually at work on Monday morning?"

"You know I am," he said. "You know everything about me."

"Used to," she said. "You surprised me today, though, so maybe I don't know you as well as I thought."

"You never used to like getting up early," Bradley resisted the impulse to smooth the hair behind Melissa's neat little ears.

"I used to make you breakfast," she said.

Bradley's fingers itched to touch her. Melissa was one of those women who don't seem to have pores in their skin it was so smooth. Bradley noticed things like this—he worked in an ad agency.

Bradley sat next to her. "My car didn't work today," he said.

"Yeah, I know," Melissa's voice held a hint of regret. "Sorry about that."

"Does that mean you wanted to see me?" he asked.

"How would I know you would come to this park, *my* park? I've never seen you here before."

Bradley nodded. "How curious. But maybe not a coincidence." The doves scattered as he leaned forward and took her hand.

Other Married People

I first met Jack when I was sixteen and working as a carhop. He drove in one day in a purple Camaro. His dad owned the local Chevy dealership. What a car! All curves and yummy lines, just the right size and low to the ground. That purple car made me swoon.

"You like my wheels," he said when I came to take his order.

"Yup," I said.

"What about me?"

"The truth?" I chewed on my pencil. "I didn't even see you. Just the car. My favorite color. My favorite size."

"Your favorite flavor too?" He was flirty as hell.

"Funny," I said. "What do you want to eat?"

His eyebrows shot up and I just knew he was going to keep going with the trite comments: *a little of what you're having* or *just you honey* or *how about a little sugar?* I dug my nails into my fist, the one not gripping the order pad. I was in a mood to let him have it.

"Just a milkshake." He thought a minute. "Vanilla."

"Good choice," I said and spun around to head back to the kitchen. I stole a look back at that car. "Camaro," I said aloud. Dreamy.

After that, he had come by about once a week. Sure, he asked me out. But the car was a stumbling block. It was hard to even see what his face was like when he was in it—the purple swooped me up every time. I only saw myself driving that car.

The next year I headed off to the university with a group of my friends on the Minnesota border in Grand Forks. In his junior year Jack transferred to the agricultural college, also on the border, but farther south, Fargo.

I forgot about him but sure didn't lose the car. I asked my dad for one that first Fall. "When you get a job, you can have one," he said, handing me the keys to the Impala he had bought for me second hand. It was wide-bodied and blue, not my type at all.

Five years later, I was behind the counter of the pharmacy in Crookston when a tall, lanky guy with a ponytail came up to the till. "Janice. Janice Straight?"

"Yes," I was cautious. Seeing a woman handling drugs affected some men like an aphrodisiac.

"Jack. Jack Bergstrom. Purple Camaro. We went to high school together."

"Not exactly. You were two years older." I squinted and saw that color, brighter than eggplant. "Mr. Camaro!"

"Yeah." He sounded a little down.

"Still have it?" I thought I might offer him a good price for it.

"Nuh-uh. Totaled it in college. Icy road, not my fault."

I rang him up and handed him the bag. A month's supply of Valium. He looked hopeful as I handed him his change. Thing was, if you don't stand out as much as your car, what kind of a man does that make you?

"What time are you done here?" Jack asked, pulling his shoulders back.

"You have a car?" I stalled for time.

"Yeah." He pointed out the window to a midnight-blue Corvette. Shiny, smooth as Häagen-Dazs vanilla.

My mouth watered. "Come by at nine."

He sauntered off. I watched him fold his long legs into the low belly of that gorgeous beast. Well, hot damn, I thought.

~

"It's not too late," Jack announced six years later as we were leaving the church where we were supposed to get married. But didn't. Because he had had a panic attack five minutes after the organist began playing. I told my mother not to hire an organist. "They're gloomy," I said. "It's too *Phantom of the Opera*. Jeez, why not a string quartet?"

My mother flipped her hand back and forth in the "whatever" way she had. So infuriating. "Your father and I had an organ playing the wedding procession at our wedding. What's wrong with a little tradition?"

Why had I given in to her? Because arguing with her is like being on a bicycle with a monster SUV bearing down on you, that's why. You're not going to win, and you'll get bloodied and lame in the process.

Jack and I were in the car and headed down Washington Street. "Not too late? Not too late? Thanks a lot. You're the one who called it off." I turned my head to the left and seized on the sight of his fleshy nose, which twitched. He looked like he was going to sneeze. Was he allergic to marriage?

"What am I doing in this car with you? Why am I here when you sabotaged my—*our*—wedding?" I pressed my back against the door, shrinking as far from Jack as I could.

Jack stomped down on the accelerator as if to prevent me from bailing out right here—one mile from the church, about even with Frank's Flowers, which had occupied that spot since at least 1960.

"You didn't drive us. I did. That's why you're in this car," Jack said reasonably, his brown hair flopping over his forehead in a way I once found endearing.

He turned onto First Street. "Look it's not too late. Let's elope."

"We just left fifty people standing at Our Savior's Church. Elope! What about all those flowers, the wedding dinner my parents had catered, what about . . ."

"Janice, Janice," Jack said, pulling over to the curb. "Don't you see, it was all too much. Is that what you wanted?"

My back sagged back into the seat. A memory of the first stentorian notes of the organist filtered back to me. The organist had about six hairs on his head, all combed to one side. I started to giggle.

"What? Are you getting hysterical?"

I laughed louder. "That man. Did you see how big his feet were crunching down on those pedals? It was like Sherman's march to the sea."

Jack laughed a bit, kind of ha, ha, as if not sure he was allowed. I leaned toward him and plucked the red rose out of his jacket. I tore off each petal, reciting: "He loves me, he loves me not, he loves me . . ."

"Stop that." He hiccupped as a laugh came out of his throat in spite of his efforts.

I picked up my bouquet from the floor where I had tossed it and opened my window. "He loves me!" I shrieked, tossing out a white carnation. "He does not love any of you!" I threw out two more carnations—orange this time. "Come on Jack, join the party."

Jack took off his morning coat. "Hate this thing!" he crowed. "It's too tight, I'm too loose!" He took a white lily from my dwindling bouquet. "Juliet, Juliet, wherefore art ya Juliet?" He shredded the lily.

"Wait, wait. Remember that old expression 'gild the lily'?"

"Doesn't that mean a woman of a certain age pretending to be young?" Jack guffawed then. He was thirty, I was twenty-eight. It was easy at this point to make fun.

"Lipstick on a pig!" I hollered.

At that, we collapsed in each other's arms, tears coming out of our eyes. The ha ha's came so fast they became hums.

"Let's just go back home," I said.

"You don't want to elope?" Jack's voice was all gravelly from laughing too much. "I don't know, maybe we just—"

"—don't like married people!" I cried, lifting my hands as the weight of the wedding slipped through the open window and floated away like a balloon.

How Did You Know It Was Time to Go?

Indiana, 1974

The call came at 3:00 a.m. "Can you come and get us?" a male voice breathed in my ear.

The phone was cold in my hand. "What?"

"It's Jeff. Laurel and I are stranded on the highway. Can you pick us up?"

Shit. It was December and below freezing, the roads a glaze of ice. Central Indiana is a fog factory in the winter. I couldn't just leave them out on the highway in the middle of the night, even though all I wanted to do was cover my ears with the quilt and imagine I had dreamed the call. "Okay. Let me write down where you are."

Twenty minutes later, I pulled off I-65 about ten minutes south of West Lafayette.

Out of the fog came Jeff, big and bouncy as always, and a furious-faced Laurel.

"He drove us off the road," she said.

Jeff put his arm around her. "Fucking truck came out of nowhere. Lucky we weren't near a bridge. Good ditch right here."

"Good ditch?" Laurel stepped away from him. Her brows shot up; her mouth turned down. "Good ditch?" She had a PhD, but her vocabulary had shrunk to two words. She made a funny buzzing sound in her throat.

"Get in. Quick. Before you turn to ice." I leaned over and opened the passenger door, but Laurel got in the back and locked both doors.

Jeff slid in front with me and lifted his shoulders. "Bad mood," he whispered.

As I drove back to town, Jeff chattered about what a great time they had had in Indianapolis. "Laurel, tell Katie about the play." Silence. He tried again: "I think she'd like to hear about it." After he waited a few seconds,

79

he added: "Laurel, remember that great *silence* right before the end? Never heard anything like it." He began to laugh. "Ha, that's funny, right?"

I tapped his left kneecap with my right hand and then made a horizontal slicing motion. I imagined their relationship unspooling like a can of film, left for dead on the cutting room floor. Jeff just smiled, then started jiggling his leg and singing "Riders on the Storm."

We managed to get back to their apartment, the car floating on Laurel's rage as if we drifted atop a helium balloon, Jeff playing air guitar and rocking out, all two hundred twenty-five pounds of him. I was glad for the fog. The murk kept my eyes on the road.

At that point Jeff and Laurel had been together for six months. He was twenty-two, she was forty-six. She had jettisoned two children and a sad husband for graduate school. Why did I assume her ex was sad? Because Laurel was such a knockout—dark hair, white skin, an Anne Sexton lookalike—and really smart. There was no subject she couldn't ace. She was a crab and a curmudgeon to be sure. But also attractive in that way that some people can't resist—so hard to please, that if you managed to get her approval you felt like you had touched the moon. Jeff could never resist reaching for the moon.

I suspected that appealing to a woman twice his age was like catnip to someone like him. Jeff was smart and funny, fat, manic. And did I say sweet? Something sad in his past too.

I met Jeff by accident. My partner, Susan, was taking a class from Laurel—an organizational communication seminar. Susan came home having met her graduate cohort for the MA in the first fall seminar, all enthusiastic about Laurel, who was already a legend—the golden girl in the Purdue Comm Department. You know the story already: she had been the star in her PhD class, and even though there was a strict policy against hiring graduates of the program, Laurel had gotten a tenure track position in the same department, right after the dissertation.

Some people get a free pass. When I was an undergraduate in theater, we made jokes about students—men as well as women—doing time in a little room with a big couch when they got great roles we didn't think they deserved. I couldn't help but wonder about Laurel . . . Yes, she was supersmart but, really, how had Laurel sidestepped the no-graduates-of-Purdue rule to be hired at Purdue? I wanted to know who Laurel knew and how.

Jeff and I met because Susan was so smitten by Laurel. "She's so brilliant!" she would say or, with a wistful air, "Laurel is so worldly!" Then, inevitably, "She's so beautiful. I can't believe she's forty-six." Somehow the four of us ended up going to the movies or going out for drinks or dinner. Susan cornered Laurel in an engrossing conversation every time we were anywhere. That's how I got to know Jeff. We were left alone, staring at each other, the first time the four of us went out. He cast his clear blue eyes my way and I opened up.

I told you Jeff was heavyset and kind of quirky, but every detail about him—his floppy hair always two haircuts behind, his huge square physique (he had to have been over six three), his goofy grin and bad jokes—was endearing to me. At first I thought of him as kind of a brother figure. Later I wondered if that was way off base. Because I found him attractive too.

One night I said to Susan, "Do you think we have crushes on these people?"

Susan had been wolfing down a pepperoni pizza in our tiny apartment living room. Two, three, four slices disappeared in rapid succession before she pushed her plate away. "What?" she said. "You must be kidding. She's so gorgeous, I can't figure out why she's with him."

"I think he's handsome," I replied. "So that makes my point. You like Laurel. I guess maybe I like Jeff. Maybe. Or maybe not."

"You are so fucked up." Susan snatched a crust from her plate and leveled it at me like a pointer. "I can't believe you think he's good-looking. On what planet?"

I took the last leftover shred of pepperoni and popped it in my mouth. Susan glared at me. A giggle erupted as I chewed. Susan choked as she swallowed, her eyes popping out at me and tearing up a little. But then we both sniggered in that helpless way you do when you think you're pissed off but the argument is really too hilarious even to you.

"We are so fucked up!" she gasped.

So that was the end of that. Except for how right she was that things were rocky between us.

"I guess I don't think Laurel is so beautiful," Susan said with a sigh. "I mean I think I thought that, but somehow, now, I mean, what is she doing with him? It's kind of repulsive to think about."

"Yeah, what is he doing with her?" I said. "It IS repulsive."

That was the beginning of when things got interesting.

~

After the night I rescued Jeff and Laurel from the highway, Jeff started calling me when he was on late shift at the nursing home where he worked. He was a male orderly before there were any—medical facilities were mostly female domains then, except for doctors and surgeons. He would usually begin: "Got a few minutes?"

Susan was never home—she would flee to her late graduate seminars followed by intense bar talk. Sometimes I would go, other times I would stay home. I was grinding out my thesis and applying to doctoral programs. I guess you could say boredom edged out any excitement left in my thesis topic: an analysis of three solo performances. I had loved the productions, swooned at meeting the actresses, but now I had to make a case for "performance as research," as my advisor back in Evanston always called it. Something about the "r" word made me feel like I had carpal tunnel every time I sat at the trusty IBM Selectric.

So, when Jeff called and asked if I had a few, I would always say: "God yes!"

He had the kind of mind that roved—around the globe, through the encyclopedia of philosophy—he had moved from Descartes to Diderot in one week. He was happy scrutinizing minutiae too, things like the public records of faculty salaries in Laurel's department or the amount of chemicals used in the campus lily pond. Nothing got past him.

So when he started talking about his relationship all the time, I paid attention. "Laurel doesn't like my paisley shirts anymore," he announced one day. "She thinks they make me look fat."

Jeff had a blue paisley shirt that matched his knockout blue eyes. "Bummer," I said, lingering on the two syllables with sympathy.

Laurel was skinny and tall—the coat hanger figure of a model. "Hard to trust people with no flesh," my father always said. When I asked him why, he would say, "Think about it. Not much there." I always found that argument compelling, but then I always had at least five pounds to burn. Kind of a reserve battery pack if I needed it.

But fashion was the least of Jeff's worries. "Laurel's finally getting a divorce," he said one night.

"Oh? I thought that was behind her." I wondered why she didn't have the kids if everything was final, not even on weekends.

Jeff kind of hummed into the phone. "You know, Katie, I hope you don't think I'm a creep, but when I met Laurel I kind of liked that she was married—separated but married—you know?"

I thought for the umpteenth time about the twenty-four years that separated them. "Well, yeah, sure." Susan and I were the exact same age, and I didn't think that was so great either. We were always going through the same stuff at the same time: insecurity about graduate school, or parents who hated our majors in college, or, early on, who would make our fake IDs so we could get into the bars. Lately I couldn't remember why it had seemed like a good idea to move in with her. She was obsessed with Purdue, and I was obsessed with leaving West Lafayette. The location thing lurked on the surface, but really, we didn't spend any time together alone anymore. Funny how a relationship can slide from lovers into housemates by inches. Then that slow-growing elephant in the living room suddenly inflates and you crash into it.

Jeff had some substance issues. Well, it was 1974, lots of us did. The problem was that he worked in a medical facility. The night shift. He dispensed the before-bed meds and sometimes the early-bird ones too. The meds cabinet at Memorial wasn't even locked, not that a padlock or a tricky combination would have stopped Jeff. This is the man who read all the greats in Western Philosophy in one semester, remember—or at least Wittgenstein to Nietzsche. What does that have to do with locks and keys? Just think about it.

He had called at 1:00 a.m. for maybe five weeks in a row to tell me how Laurel's divorce was coming along.

"Seems slow," I said. "Even for someone who's ambivalent."

I could almost hear Jeff's ears perk up at the other end of the line. "You think Laurel's ambivalent?"

Careful, I told myself, don't backpedal too fast. "Well, she's got the two kids she doesn't have custody of, right?"

"Uh-huh."

"That's kind of hard. Unless she doesn't like kids." I paused, waiting for Jeff to interject on her behalf. But he said nothing. Not right away.

Then, finally, he said: "She's got me."

I wondered if that was supposed to be funny. Jeff wasn't your average twenty-two-year-old. He was an old soul. I forgot to mention that Kierkegaard was his favorite thinker. Or maybe it was the I-Thou guy, whose name I always confused with someone else. Not Bergson, the other one.

"I don't think you qualify," was all I said.

"Anyway, I think it's stressing her out. She doesn't seem herself."

"Moody?" I suggested.

"I guess I'd call it demanding. Doesn't want me to go out without her, that kind of thing."

"So, I guess work is one of the few places you're by yourself," I said, half joking.

"Yeah, these people have so much Demerol and morphine in them they're not here. They're worse than not here."

"Gosh, what's that, do you think, worse than not here?"

"I'd say it's wanting not to be here at all." His voice had a grim note I hadn't heard before.

"Hey, Jeff, everything okay with you?" I had been doodling by the phone, a kind of half-monster, half-crab looking thing scuttling off the page. I dropped my pen and gripped the phone a little tighter.

"Shit," he said. "Gotta go. The light in 12B is on again. Poor woman thinks it's Sunday and her son is coming. But she doesn't have a son, and I'm not sure she's going to see Sunday ever again."

He clicked off. Susan was out again that night. Some kind of work-study group Laurel led for a few of the MA candidates. I was beginning to have my doubts about the work part. The study part too. I wished I could drive over to the nursing home to find Jeff, but I didn't think that would be okay. Jeff had pretty strict boundaries about his job. Maybe because it was the only thing in his life that was his, just his.

I spent another hour trying to focus on a new outline for the last chapter of my thesis. Then Susan came slinking into the living room. When she saw me, she tried for perky. "Oh, you're still up!"

"Yeah, lots to do."

Susan lurched into the kitchen. I heard a clunk, then a muffled "fuck" as she opened the refrigerator door. She reappeared with a cold piece of pizza. It looked a little wrinkled, like it had been lonely on the shelf for too long. "Want anything?" she said. She seemed a little down.

"How was group?" I asked.

"Not good. Laurel couldn't focus, so we went out for a couple of beers after."

"Hmm." I wondered why she hadn't called and invited me to join them but didn't say so.

"Problems with Jeff," Susan said. "Poor Laurel." She took a deep breath and shook her head, trying for that tough-girl actress look from those gritty '60s movies she loved to watch.

"What do you mean 'poor Laurel'? I'd say she has a good deal with him. He's very good to her."

"He's so immature," Susan said in a knowing way. She plopped down in a tattered beige recliner, something an old love had left behind, and put her feet up. "Stop defending him. You know perfectly what I mean."

I pushed the pad of paper I had been writing on away. First I said, "I'm getting a beer," which I did. Then I came back into the living room. "Tell me what you're talking about."

"Come on, Katie. Laurel's a sophisticated older woman. She knows something about the world. She's been places. Now she's stuck in Lafayette, Indiana."

The being stuck in Indiana I could really relate to, but I just said, "And that's Jeff's fault how?" I wished I were the kind of person who could drink a beer in one gulp and then crush the can with one hand.

"You don't get it, so I'm not going to bother."

~

As Susan became more focused on Laurel, Laurel did not reciprocate. Or, I should say, she simply homed in tighter on Jeff. His calls came almost every night now.

"I miss my old life," he said.

"Tell me." I missed my old life too, the one where I was in my own graduate classes and I never waited up for Susan. I had received an assistantship in the fall to start a PhD in San Diego. It couldn't come soon enough. Coming to central Indiana to finish my thesis hadn't been my brightest idea. I felt like a faculty wife, except Susan wasn't faculty.

"Katie," his voice was tense. "I'm kind of scared, if you want to know." He rushed on. "The divorce is final next month. But Laurel is over that. She's already talking about our wedding."

"What? Don't you have a say in that?"

"Yeah, you'd think. But she assumes it's a done deal already. She's already signing my last name when she sends out a note to her parents, for instance."

"Corcoran? She's calling herself Laurel Corcoran?"

I could hear a helpless shrug in his voice. Then a deep in-breath. Jeff was smoking, something stronger than cigarettes, at work.

"I'm feeling a little pushed," he said.

"Yeah." I chewed on a hangnail. I knew I could urge him to resist, but what was the use? We all seemed to have someone in our lives we just couldn't say no to. "Look, why don't I meet you at the Home? We'll go out for some fries."

"Good idea," he said.

But when I pulled into the parking lot of Memorial Nursing Home, under the lone blue parking lot light, his red Jeep was gone.

~

Susan moped into the kitchen one morning. "Laurel tells me she and Jeff are getting married."

My hand froze on the tea kettle. "For real?"

Susan pushed her short blond hair straight up from her forehead. Her gray eyes darted around the room. "For real."

"Well, I guess we saw this coming," I said. "If we'd been looking."

"I don't get it." Susan rummaged in a cupboard, pulled out a granola bar, and headed back to our bedroom. "I'm not going to class today. I think I'm coming down with something."

Susan recovered enough to go to Laurel's seminar that evening. Later on, Jeff called and told me he was thinking of leaving town. "My dad's really lonely now that my mom's gone," he said.

"I forget when she died . . .?"

"Well, it's been ten years. But he seems to be getting a lot worse. Drinking too much bourbon. There's not much to do in southern Ohio."

"Kind of like central Indiana," I said, thinking of my own parents up in the Dakotas. They had each other, though, and they actually seemed to like dancing at places like the Elks Club. All their friends did too, and they went out a lot.

"Their part of Ohio," Jeff pointed out, "borders Appalachia. It's scary quiet. Except when someone gets bonked on the head for stealing a pig."

Jeff's voice had a dreamy, stoned quality. I had to laugh. "Your dad's a doctor or something, right?"

"Dentist. I guess I'm not really representing his life very well."

"So," I looked up at the crappy chandelier in our apartment. "I'd really miss you if you moved."

"You're leaving in three months yourself."

Do you know those moments, when if you just said something simple, like "I wouldn't mind a road trip to Ohio," the planets would shift and whirl a little faster? Or even slower. It doesn't matter what you'd say, but something would happen.

But before I could make my proposal, Jeff started coughing and kind of retching. "Katie, could you come over here now? I think I'm having some kind of attack."

I didn't leave Susan a note. Just grabbed my peacoat and headed for my car.

The Home wasn't far, about twelve minutes. Next door to it was the West Lafayette Hospital. An emergency van sat in the circular drive, its lights blinking. I put my hand to my chest, thinking of Jeff hacking as we talked. I waited, but no one came out of the van on a stretcher.

I pushed through the double doors of the Home and walked down a long tan hallway with shining floors. The cleaner had just polished them, but you could see the scratches under the smooth surface. Many feet had shuffled along these floors, marking the sad grooves of a pathway to nowhere.

Jeff's wing was on the third floor. I climbed the stairs, the steps so close together I managed three at a time, then walked by the nurse's station. No one was there.

When I had been in this building before, it had a kind of hum. People snoring, food carts clattering down corridors, aides laughing in the cafeteria over evening snacks. Lights going off, a displaced yell or two. It was about eleven thirty and too quiet.

I finally ran into an aide in the hallway by the cafeteria. "Excuse me, I'm looking for Jeff Corcoran."

She set her lips to one side in a wary way. "You know he's supposed to be working tonight. Well, he *was* working tonight."

"Yeah, I talked to him on the phone a little while ago. Is he okay?"

"I don't know. I guess."

"Well, he was kind of having an asthma attack or something and I was worried about him. I'm a close friend. My name's Katie. Katie Robb."

She gave me that look again, her dark eyes sizing me up. "Yeah, I think I've heard of you. I'm Marty."

We stared at each other for a while. I was about to go when she said: "We could check the dispensary. He was due to give the nighttime meds." She motioned for me to follow her. She slid along the floor, her white sneakers making a shushing sound. "I'm not supposed to take you there," she said.

"Well, thanks. Really."

The dispensary was a small room, about eight by twelve, with shelves and two fridges and a wide assortment of bottles and pills behind glass cupboard doors that were so old they just had brass fasteners to keep them shut.

"This is the last place I saw him."

I imagined Jeff grabbing a fistful of pill bottles and pouring them down his throat, having a seizure, then lying on his back in the middle of the room, fading away until he was gone.

Panicked that I had missed too many clues for too long, I asked: "You're sure he didn't have an accident tonight? Have to go to the hospital next door?"

"Ah, no, I think I would have noticed the commotion. You can check in Emergency if you're concerned."

"Okay."

"Look . . . Katie. I think Jeff might be sick. But not that sick."

"Oh?" The arches of my feet went a little rubbery. I put an arm out against the wall to steady the wobble.

"Yeah. I think he just had to go. Leave. You know." Marty shrugged. "Gotta go."

I followed her out the door.

"You look like you need a coffee." She pointed to a doorway two doors down.

The cafeteria reminded me of elementary school, small tan chairs and tables, dirty-brown linoleum floor. It was empty too. I wondered if a seismic jolt had flashed through the roof and vaporized all the people in the place.

I scuffed around the tables for a few minutes, hoping for a sign that Jeff had spent time there that evening. About the time I thought about going next door to check to see if Jeff was in the hospital, I spotted Jeff's green backpack lying under a table. I made a beeline for it as if it were King Solomon's mine.

Jeff loved this backpack, covered with old campaign stickers, including one for McGovern in 1972, and it usually bulged with a week's worth of stuff. When I lifted it, it felt uncharacteristically light. That had to be Jeff's first clue for me: travel spare. When I opened it, there was a square of paper written in pencil: *Katie, sorry, it was time to go. There's never a good way to leave, is there? I don't mean you. I'll call you, later on. You can count on it. Don't show this to anyone. J.*

A paperback book was inside. One of Jeff's favorite thinkers. Not Bergson, the other one: Martin Buber. *I and Thou.* Of course. I figured that was the second message: go only with connection, the real thing. Nothing else mattered.

∼

I didn't want to go home but I had nowhere else to go. I came into the apartment, the green backpack over one shoulder. I grabbed a Miller Lite from the refrigerator.

Susan was sprawled in her antique recliner, eating a chicken leg. She had taken her contacts out and was wearing square wire-rimmed glasses.

"How was class?"

"Class?" She looked at me as if my head was missing. "It's midnight. I can barely remember an hour ago. Class was over at eight."

"Well, I left here around eleven. You weren't here."

"God, I was listening to Laurel talk about the kind of wedding she wants this time. The first one was such a bust, she said."

"Um. I know you think Jeff's a bust, too."

"She'll wake up one day," Susan said, stretching her mouth open for a big bite. "She'll see he's just not for her."

"Yeah, maybe." Susan's hair looked like she had been hacking at it with her nail scissors again.

"No maybe about it." Susan chewed as if it were her righteous duty.

I wanted to say, "And you'll be waiting, just for that moment," but I focused on my beer.

She just smiled as if I had agreed with her.

I just sat on the couch, sipping from the can and watching Susan gnaw on the chicken leg until she tossed it on the coffee table. A thread of gristle hung from the knuckle.

That was when I realized that this poor excuse for a conversation had nothing to do with Laurel or Jeff. It was all about us. Susan thought I was dull and immature, and that she, like Laurel, was entitled to something and someone else. And I didn't want to think much about her at all. Susan's glasses glinted in the dim room; her eyes behind them looked red and irritated.

"So why doesn't she just move on right now?" I said, calculating how much rent I could afford on my own, if I could keep up with my car insurance, and how much money I would have to try to borrow from my dad if I left Susan. When I left Susan.

Susan just looked at me with bleary eyes. I put the beer can down, half empty. "I'm going to bed," I said, and I walked out, leaving Susan to dream of changing her hairstyle, her clothes, her address, to something more like the fantasy world she and Laurel were waltzing in together.

EXHIBIT C

Pale Blue

Your mother tells you secrets have to be earned, but sometimes you look down at your feet and see one lying in plain sight.

When you're ten years old, you rush home from school and collect the mail from the floor in the hallway by the front door. You love the sound of letters spilling on the wood floor—at four o'clock they enter the life of the house, sliding from the chapped hands of the postman into the brass slot in the front door. Then, at five-thirty each afternoon your father comes home from work, takes the mail off the hall table, and sorts it into piles.

On most days, he goes upstairs and takes off his jacket and tie, puts on a sweater or a T-shirt in the summer. He comes back downstairs, takes the newspaper into the living room, sits in the big brown upholstered chair, and slips off his slippers—you wonder why he bothers changing out of his dress shoes upstairs when he's just going to take the shoes off again. Then he hides his face in the paper.

But on this day, you notice that he picks up one letter and slips it into his coat pocket. It doesn't go into any of the piles. You noticed that letter earlier in the day, a blue envelope written in a child's block printing, the letters slanting to the left so the words are hard to read. Your own writing looks a little like it—maybe the person who wrote the letter is a girl who is the same age as you are. She has honey-colored hair, too, just like you. You see her small face grow serious as she licks the envelope and carries it to a post box on the corner of her street. She looks to the left and right, reaches out and pulls open the mail drawer—she's just a little bit taller than the mailbox—and drops it in.

When you ask your father who sent the letter, he looks at you with his steady gray eyes. "Just someone," he says. "Someone I used to know."

That can't be true. It's not just someone he used to know—he still knows this person or he wouldn't be getting a letter. The envelopes are always light blue and small, and very thin—you suspect they contain a single sheet of paper. Your fingers itch to open one. What if this girl somewhere is a girl just like you, stuck in a small town, waiting for her father to come back? Because your father goes away too and you kind of hold your breath until he comes back. It seems to you that every time your father receives one of these letters, he leaves for two, three, four days, and once a whole week. Each time you are afraid he'll never return.

And then the thing you're afraid of does happen. Your father goes away for a week but then he doesn't come home. You ask your mother: "When is he coming back?"

Your mother's name is April, like springtime. She has dark-brown hair with a streak of gray at the crown. She is in the kitchen making a chicken stew; in her hand is a large spoon. She stirs something in the pot in front of her and then she stops. "What did you say?"

You sit on the high stool at the counter in the kitchen so you can watch her cook. "When is he coming back?"

She sighs and sets the spoon on a shallow yellow plate next to the stove. "I don't know where he is."

You squirm on the stool. You hold on to the counter and count to ten. When you speak your voice sounds a little high and breathy, but you can still talk. "That can't be true. He goes away, he says because of business, every month. You must know where he goes."

Your mom looks at you, but she seems far away, like someone else's mom named April. Her blue eyes are flat and watery. "He travels for work. He just tells me the name of the city."

You slump forward on the counter. Your eyes feel watery too and you rub the skin under them to wipe away the damp. "What city?"

"Chicago," she says very quietly. She puts her hand on the counter and takes hold of your wrist. Her hand is soft and smooth; it brings her closer. She is your mom, not someone else. You take a deep breath and touch her hand with a fingertip. She smiles at you and her mouth twists a little. Her face with its broad cheekbones is very dear, a face you trust.

"I love you, Marcy," she says. Don't ever forget that."

She seems sad and you wonder if she has a secret too. You think back to the pale blue envelopes; you try to remember the return address. Was it Chicago? You've never been there but you've seen it on a map. You live in southern Indiana, not so far away. "Can we go to the library?"

The library is one of your favorite places, five blocks from your house. Sometimes you go by yourself but this time your mother takes you. Shadows from the oak trees that line the streets fall onto the sidewalk like tiny hands. It's fall and the leaves glow orange and red, so bright that you imagine that if it were dark, the leaves would still burn the air. A squirrel runs in front of you and leaps with a crooked hop into a tree. You skip for a few steps and feel light and free like the squirrel.

You and your mom cross the five streets, then walk up the three steps into the library. She turns right into the fiction section, and you go left to wander around the reference room, the shelves stacked almost to the ceiling. Lucky for you, you find the book you need on one of the lower shelves, about architecture in Chicago, and you read that some of the greatest architects in the world lived there once, people like Louis Sullivan and Frank Lloyd Wright. You study the photographs of their buildings and think their shapes and styles are different from anything you've ever seen. Sullivan was the father of the modern skyscraper and built the Auditorium Building where the Chicago Symphony first played. It was grand and solid, the largest building at the time in the whole country. Wright's houses don't reach upward like Sullivan's do. They hug the earth, spreading out low and flat and wide.

You study the pictures and you make a decision. You think the little girl who wrote the letters lives in a house like the Wright houses—she sits at a long oak table in front of a huge stone fireplace. She has a blue pad of paper and matching envelopes. She writes to your father with a black pen and tears off the top sheet of the pad when she's done and puts it into the envelope. Her face is round and earnest; she bites her bottom lip with tiny white teeth.

You sit down at a table in the library and take out your notebook. You start writing a letter to your father. "Dear Dad, I wish you'd come home. Mom misses you. I miss you. I went into your bedroom when Mom was gone and looked at your clothes. You know that nice brown suit you have with the tiny red stripes, the one you always wear with a red tie? That suit is gone. And so is your gray cardigan sweater, the one that's kind of shaggy and sometimes snags my fingernails so that the threads pucker. I think at least two pairs of your shoes are missing. Did you pack a big bag?

"Will you send me a letter and tell me that you're all right and when you're coming back? I have a set of new paints, blue and orange and red, and I'm drawing something special. Let me know if you'd like me to send it to you."

But then you realize you don't know the address to put on the letter. You seal it up in a blue envelope you took from your mother's desk and brought with you. Then, you begin to write in big block letters that slant backward. You print your father's name: Frank Jacobs. Then you write: Chicago. Then you put the letter under a pile of books. You need to figure out how your father can get this message from you.

You pick up your stack of books and the letter and go into a small room in the library with big cushiony chairs. The walls are wood paneled and a painting of a man in a black suit and round glasses leans out from the wall. On one wall is a plaque that says: *Reading Room*. You sit down in a red chair that feels like corduroy and you put your books and your envelope on the small table next to the chair.

You squeeze your eyes shut and imagine you're walking through a doorway and then another one. You glide down a hall like in a dream toward a third doorway. This one opens onto a street in Chicago. You walk up to a remarkable house in the center of the block, a Frank Lloyd Wright house, long with a flat roof and windows that have lead designs in them. By the front door is a number: 534. As you stand there, you can see inside that house, but nobody can see you watching.

The other little girl is sitting at her kitchen table, bending over a pad of paper. The walls in the room are yellow. You sneak down the hallway to the dining room and peer into the living room. You like the fireplace that takes up almost one wall. You have to tear yourself away from exploring the house to return to the kitchen where the little girl is. After lunch, the girl walks out the front door and past the sign that says 534 to the street corner to mail her letter. The street sign at the corner says Sayre Ave.

The girl on the street starts to shrink like when you're looking out the wrong end of a telescope, and you open your eyes to find you're back in the red chair in the library. You wonder if the red chair was a magic chair that took you where you needed to go and then brought you back.

You take your envelope out from under the stack of books, and you write on the line after your father's name: 534 Sayre Avenue. And on the next line, you print: Chicago, Illinois. On the way home from the library, you mail the letter in the corner mailbox near your house.

Your mom smiles and asks, "Who are you writing to?"

"It's a secret," you say.

In a few days you're sure the envelope will arrive in Chicago. A postman will put your letter into his bag and walk down the streets that are his special route. Your letter will slide through a slot in the front door on Sayre Avenue and land on the hall floor. And in the afternoon, when he comes into the house, your father will find a blue envelope that has special printing on it, and he'll put it into his pocket. Someone might ask him who sent it, but he won't tell. "No one you know," he'll say. But he knows who wrote the letter. He'll read it and maybe then he'll have to go away for three days, or four, or a week, to visit his other little girl.

Standing in the Light

Ten minutes early to meet her friend Vee for coffee, Marla captured a table for two in the back of the café. She began to read a novel on the Kindle app on her phone. Marla's new novel had just come out, and she had been paired with another writer, the author of a book called *Alternate Endings*, to do a Zoom interview. She had felt compelled to read the other writer's book before the event not only to be collegial but because the title had snagged her attention. After fifty pages she had concluded that the title might be the highlight of the book.

Distracted, she raised her head. Vee had rushed in the door and stood impatiently in the ordering line. Marla waved. Vee grinned at her, flipping her scarf over her shoulder and hitching her hip in a movie star pose. Just as Marla gratefully tossed her phone into her purse—*goodbye endings, hello beginnings*, she thought aimlessly—she heard a young woman at a nearby table say to another: "My mom doesn't get it that her generation is no longer the one standing in the light."

Marla turned to see the woman's companion nod knowingly. The voice continued on, its freight of self-importance and sarcasm weighing in about equally: "God. Sometimes I just want to say, stand back! Give me some air!"

"Yeah, like isn't it time to be the support staff and not the star?" the other woman said, her head bobbing like a tiny boat on a rough sea.

Marla looked around the room, each wall painted a different color (her chair backed up to the purple wall). Most of the tables wobbled. It was easy to make the case that she was the oldest person in the coffee shop. Except for Vee of course. The two younger women had dropped their voices. Thankfully, Marla could no longer make out what they were saying.

"How old do you think those two are?" Marla asked Vee when she sat opposite her.

"Wait. No hug? No 'How fantastic to see you my friend'? Not even after we haven't met for two weeks?" Vee half stood and leaned over the table to deposit a smack on Marla's cheek. "I'm glad to see *you* anyway," she said.

Then Vee craned her neck to check out the two women behind them. "Well, a lot younger than we are." She scanned the room and made a face. "That wouldn't be hard here. I guess." She wrinkled her nose and let loose with her usual half snark of a giggle.

Vee smoothed her curls away from her forehead. "But guess what? We don't care!"

Her friend straightened her shoulders, looking so triumphant that Marla began to laugh. And laugh. A tear trickled toward her nose. "Thanks. I needed that."

"So, when did you get so fussy about a little age?" Vee dipped her finger around the edge of her latte and sucked off the foam. Her blue eyes squinted at Marla—she had forgotten her glasses again.

Marla stopped laughing. "I guess when a friend of a friend I was hiking with the other day actually said, for real: "Seventy is the new sixty!"

"Oh no—hasn't she seen that *New Yorker* cartoon where the grizzled guy sits with another geezer at the bar and the first one says to the other: 'Seventy isn't the new anything.' They both look like they've eaten a few lemons and are starting on vinegar martinis."

Marla started to laugh again. "I guess she hadn't. And if she had, maybe she'd say: 'We don't care!'"

Vee nodded. "Okay, let's change the subject. Puh-lease. My daughter has been calling me lately to see how I am. She's checking up on me if you can believe it. Now that she's forty she knows everything and says she worries about me. For no reason that I can see. So, tell me about what you're writing. You are writing, right?"

Marla nodded. "Well, I'm kind of in a slump. The new novel is not exactly spooling out on cue."

"Hey, as long as you're thinking about it, you're writing in the larger sense, right?"

"I didn't say that, did I, to you?"

"No, I heard it somewhere. It makes a kind of sense though. How's your mom?"

"I thought you wanted to change the subject! But maybe there isn't another subject at the moment? Because Mom is turning ninety-seven in two weeks and really is doing well. But it's hard for her, you know? She says everything takes longer."

Vee bit into an apricot brioche. "She's amazing. How can you be so worried about aging when you have a model like her?"

Startled, Marla swigged a too-large and too-hot swig of coffee. "I didn't think I was until I heard those young women as I was waiting for you. I've never thought that my mother, for instance, isn't worthy of attention."

"She's very worthy! So she can't climb K2 or Everest. Is that the measure of being human?"

"Gosh, Vee, you're so profound today. Seriously. What is the measure of being human?"

Vee stirred her coffee, her eyes blinking rapidly. "Compassion?" she finally offered. "Humor?"

"Hmm." Marla pointed at the brioche on Vee's plate. "Could I have a taste?"

When Vee handed over a chunk of the pastry, Marla popped it in her mouth and chewed gratefully. "It's such a relief to talk to you. I don't know what's wrong with me that I'm letting two twentysomethings plunge me into the abyss."

"That bad? Okay, the facts. I'll admit that around sixty-five I stopped buying the fifty-pound dog food and found myself gravitating toward the twenty instead. Or even fifteen. Do you know what I'm saying?"

"I do," Marla said.

"But isn't something like that a sensible adaptation and not a very big thing? I mean, if you sprain your ankle, don't you minimize how often you go up the stairs? Aging is like that. You have to get smarter about how you use your body. Or maybe more realistic. But isn't it okay?"

Marla suddenly felt like crying. "I guess it isn't okay." She sniffed. "I always thought I was super strong and fast. And now in airports I notice younger people passing me when I think I'm walking briskly."

A little smile tugged at the corners of Vee's mouth. "Keep telling yourself, we don't care!" She put her hand over Marla's. "Honey, I keep thinking about your mom, about Dorothy. Who's still beautiful. And funny. I just want to cheer her on. And you know what? She's still standing in the light."

Marla lowered her head, her eyes brimming.

"Tell me what you're thinking," Vee prodded when Marla stayed silent.

Marla looked up into the kind face of her friend. "Something a little corny, I guess."

"C'mon," Vee said. "So what? My dad was always corny. And now that's what I miss the most about him. Tell me."

"Okay, I wish this café had a message board. Because I'd post this: 'The light is big enough and bright enough for all of us.'"

"Was that so hard to say? I like it." Vee tossed her curls. "Of course, bright light isn't always flattering. Think of Blanche DuBois and her little red lantern covering the bare bulb so that her suitor would see her as young."

"She wanted magic." Marla leaned closer to Vee as if imparting a secret. "A little magic helps get us through. Especially when things falter. It offers perspective. It's kind of like a good friend." She raised her cup and tilted it at Vee.

Curiosities

Near midnight, Sophie hurried past the shuttered drugstore in the dark downtown. Footsteps sounded behind her. She didn't dare look. Block after block, they echoed her stride even as she picked up her pace. By the time she passed the only café left on Main Street, long closed, she had broken into a desperate run.

A shop she had not noticed appeared at the corner of Main and Tarrant Street: *Bob's Antiques and Curiosities*. Lights of all kinds blazed in the window: old-fashioned globe lamps with dazzling colored glass, ceramic figures (some with bright halos and some lit from within), a fluorescent crescent of a moon. Winded, Sophie grabbed the door handle—which turned, to her surprise—and swung herself into the shop. An old-fashioned shade hung limply over the window of the door. She peered under the shade and anxiously checked the street before she turned around.

"Hello?" she ventured. "Is anyone here?" The door didn't have a deadbolt she could turn, just an ornate opening for an antique key, but no key hung by the door. "Hello?" she called again, her breathing rapid, still harsh in her throat. Even while Sophie appreciated a place to rest, the seemingly deserted shop unnerved her.

A dark wooden counter dominated the back of the shop, and next to it a high-backed stool. A baggy, gray cardigan, draped over the stool back, looked like its wearer had just stepped out of it.

A clock chimed, then another. A cuckoo announced the hour. An animated tiny boy in a blue suit came out of a timepiece tooting a miniature trumpet. Still disconcerted, Sophie slid onto the stool. The footsteps from the street rang in her ears.

For a moment she wondered if she should hide behind the counter, but just then a thin man with gray hair and round glasses came out of the back room. At the same time the door to the shop banged open. A large man burst into the room, the brim of his cap shadowing his face.

Sophie leaped up from the stool and flexed her knees. A self-defense course had taught her that taking space was the first thing to do. But then she stopped, her agitation dropping when she clearly saw the chaser's face and realized he was her ex-husband. Her relief was mixed with puzzlement that he had been the person following her. Why hadn't he just called out to her on the street?

"It's you!" she said. "Why didn't you say so?"

"Why were you out walking all alone and so late?" her ex, Ronnie, countered.

"My car wouldn't start."

"For Christ's sake, Sophie," he said. "I didn't mean to scare you. I just want to talk to you."

Ronnie had regular features and soft green eyes. He reached out just as Sophie leaned forward; his warm hand grazed her arm. A part of her wanted to lean against him, but it all seemed so awkward. They had fought so much that last year of their marriage. They knew they needed to make changes, but they didn't know what to do. And then Sophie lost her job and began to think leaving Smithfield was the only solution.

"Ronnie Bigelow?" The man with the round glasses said, taking a step forward and tapping Ronnie on the chest. "What are you doing here? I thought you left Smithfield ten years ago, said you'd never return."

"Hell, Mr. Goodall, I did leave. I came back two years later." Ronnie's voice turned wistful. "Right away I met someone, someone beautiful. As you can see."

Sophie adjusted her posture, suddenly self-conscious. She advanced on the man with the round glasses. "I owe you. Your shop saved me. I don't think I could have kept going for one more second." She grabbed his hand and squeezed it between both of hers. "I'm Sophie. Sophie Johnson."

The man took off his glasses and polished them on the shirttail hanging out of one side of his plaid pants. He shook her hand. "Bob Goodall. I'm pretty sure I knew your mother. Gaby Johnson? You look just like her." Bob went to a table with four chairs around it. "Why don't you sit down, and we'll see if we can figure out what's happening here."

"He scared me to death, tracking me through the streets!" Sophie blurted, although in truth she was more than a little glad to see Ronnie (and a bit curious too). She had often found his powerful body and sweet eyes reassuring. But she wasn't sure if she was ready to forgive him for frightening her.

"I just wanted to talk with you. That's all." Ronnie flung himself into a chair and yanked off his cap. His chest rose and fell, and his face flushed from exertion or embarrassment, Sophie wasn't sure which. She was glad to see she was not the only one upset by their odd and unexpected encounter.

"Now, now." Bob pulled out a chair for Sophie but addressed Ronnie. "You just get your breath . . . here, slow and deep, that's it."

Once she saw that Ronnie was calming down, Sophie focused on Bob. "Tell me how you knew my mother."

Bob had an earnest face, one of those late-middle aged men with deep grooves from nose to mouth, and crinkly skin around his washed-out blue eyes. "Well, Stephenson is my family name. You could say your mother and I were distant cousins growing up." He then proceeded to trace the lineage of Johnsons and Stephensons in a way that was confusing to Sophie, ending with "And of course your mother's mother was the half sister of my grandfather Nels, who wasn't really a Stephenson but a Halgren." A delighted smile lit up his face.

"Oh," said Sophie, stumped. "I don't remember my mother mentioning this half sister of my grandmother. I don't think." She leaned forward. "But how wonderful that you grew up together. What was she like then?"

"Excuse me," Ronnie said. "This is all just great, but I have to tell Sophie why I was following her tonight." His mouth softened in a tender way. "I'm sorry if I . . ."

"You terrified me!" she said. "Why didn't you identify yourself?"

"Why didn't you turn around and see who was behind you?" Ronnie's face, which had reverted to its usual pale hue, flamed again. "Isn't that the normal response when someone is trying to catch up to you?"

"For a man maybe, a big man like you. For a woman like me late at night walking alone? Not on your life!"

Bob Stephenson nodded. "I can see we all need a cup of tea." He rose and left the room.

Sophie looked longingly after Bob. "Such a nice man," she said.

"Sophie, I want you to come home."

"And where is that?" She turned to face Ronnie as if seeing him fully for the first time, her large brown eyes tracking his face.

"Why, on Sixth Street, where we lived together."

"You still live there? I thought you moved after we divorced." Sophie's small features rearranged themselves into a perplexed frown.

"Where would I go?" Ronnie shifted in his chair, squaring his shoulders.

"I don't know." She spoke slowly, trying to remember the last time they had talked. "But, Ronnie, I haven't lived in this town for years. I left right after we broke up. I just came back."

"I know. That's why I followed you tonight. I hadn't seen you in so long. I couldn't believe it was you. I—"

Bob returned with a tray with three cups, a small pitcher of milk, and a lovely teapot with small blue flowers across the middle. Three spoons lined one side of the tray and a bowl of sugar on the other. "I'm glad to see you two are talking to each other," he said.

Sophie calmly tipped the pot and poured hot tea into the waiting cups. "Sugar?" she asked Bob.

"Just milk. Thank you." Bob looked fondly at Sophie, at the maroon scarf tied in a complicated knot at her throat. "You do remind me of Gaby. She had style, your mother. And a big heart."

"Oh yes," Sophie said, pinching the bridge of her nose with one hand to keep back her tears. Her mother's absence filled the room. "I so miss her. I'd give anything if I could go back and see you and her when you were young. There's so much I'd like to know about my mother."

"Gaby was deep," Bob said, crossing his legs and leaning back in his chair.

Ronnie held up one hand. "Can I just say something here?"

Bob and Sophie turned their heads to face him in a movement so symmetrical it was as if they had rehearsed. Bob's mouth thinned into a straight line. "We are talking about Sophie's mother. A woman we both miss very much." His voice sounded stern and authoritative, one you'd expect from the junior high school teacher he once was. "You're interrupting. Something, I might add, you used to do in class frequently." In a more severe tone, he added: "And that was twenty years ago."

Unexpectedly, Ronnie laughed, his voice a resonant bass. "You used to be hard on me in school way back then, too: 'Pay attention, Ronnie,' you'd say. 'Time to get it together, Ronnie.'" He put his cap back on his head and squared the bill. Sophie couldn't help but admire his strong chin, the easy set of his shoulders.

Sophie twisted a button on her charcoal sweater. "Ronnie, if I promise to call you tomorrow, would that be all right?"

"You mean you want me to leave?" Disbelief echoed in Ronnie's voice. He crossed his arms tightly across his chest.

"I think that would be best," Bob said, placing a large-knuckled hand on Ronnie's solid shoulder.

"You can't walk home alone at this hour. I'll just walk back over to where I parked and bring the car around." Ronnie spoke in a measured way as he stood up. "Don't rush." He nodded at Bob. "Good seeing that there's life after teaching junior high. Nice place you got here." He backed away from them and then turned and slipped out of the door.

Sophie giggled. "He's very stubborn. But sweet too." And more handsome than she remembered, she thought.

"Yes," Bob sighed. "He means well." He glanced at the door. "Always a bit of a wild card," he said with grudging approval.

Seeing that they understood each other perfectly, Sophie sat up straighter. "I'd be grateful for anything you could tell me about Mother when she was young. I don't know why, but she only talked about the years after meeting my father. Her childhood was a blank slate. Except for her skating career."

A grin erupted on Bob's face. "She was the best ice skater this town has ever seen." Smithfield had a population of five thousand people; most likely, when Bob and Gaby were teenagers in the 1960s, it was much smaller.

"Here," he slid out of his seat. "I have some things to show you." He extended his hand, and when Sophie grasped it, led her to a covered glass case to the left of the counter. A long string hung from a floor lamp with a drooping globe and Bob pulled it, flooding the case with yellow light.

"Oh!" Sophie cupped one hand over her mouth. In front of her were seven bronze statuettes, three metal badges hung with ridged blue and red ribbon, and a series of photos. A beaded evening bag that looked identical to one of her mother's nestled in satin. "It's like a shrine." She timidly placed her index finger close to the glass. "May I—"

"Of course! Here." Bob withdrew a small key from his pocket and unlocked the case with a deft movement of his wrist. He opened the top drawer of the case, sliding the display toward them.

"What an amazing collection! Did Mom give you these?" Sophie picked up one of the bronze statuettes, of a girl gliding on skates, a scarf streaming down her back. She read the tiny writing on the base of the trophy:

Champion. 1969. Smithfield High. "She would've been just eighteen then. And you—were you in her class?"

Bob inclined his head, his eyeglasses winking in the light. "I was." He cleared his throat. "I guess that calls me out, doesn't it? I'm sixty-five."

"You don't look a day over fifty." Sophie's tone was soothing. At only thirty-five she could afford to be generous.

She had so many questions. How close had Bob been to her mother? Were they more than cousins? What was life like back then? But before she could choose which of these to ask, Bob picked up one of the ribbons. "I was her skating partner in some of the events. Of course, I wasn't the natural athlete she was. And she was a great beauty and I, well . . ."

"I'm sure you were amazing! Mom didn't put up with anything but the best, you must know that. She was . . . I guess you could say . . . *uncompromising.*" The truth was her mother had been a critical person and often directed her judgment at her only child. Remembering those admonitions— that her posture was sloppy, her clothes too drab ("and for God's sake give away that threadbare mohair sweater!"), and worse, the constant barrage of negative comments about boys she dated—deflated Sophie. But then she recalled the joy she had felt when her mother dazzled her with one of her spontaneous smiles of approval. Her mother had been such a complicated person.

Sophie replaced the trophy and selected a photo of her mother on some kind of grandstand holding a big golden cup. "I never saw her this happy." Her voice brimmed with longing.

"Here, let's just take these pictures back to the table and I'll make us a fresh pot of tea."

Seated again, Sophie began paging through the photos. Bob had disappeared to the back of the shop with the tea tray. In one picture, Gaby looked up at someone with an adoring look, her wavy auburn hair curling shoulder length, her skin smooth and radiant. Sophie pushed the bangs of her own chin-length hair back from her face. Her hair never gleamed with highlights like her mother's had. The fact was, with her green eyes and thick hair, her slender shapely figure, and her lips turned down at the corners in a Katharine Hepburn pout, her mother was just plain gorgeous. No one ever talked about her for long without mentioning it. And it wasn't just her beauty but the supple way that she moved. If Sophie shut her eyes, she could see her mother walking in that floating way she had, her favorite yellow dress swirling around her calves.

Bob returned with the tea and busied himself making hers just the way she had before, with one brown sugar cube and a bit of milk. "You didn't know your father, did you?"

"Well, you know, Mom raised me by herself." Sophie's usual defensiveness about this fell away. "Of course, you must know that."

An expression Sophie couldn't quite read flitted across Bob's face. "Yes."

"Did you know my father?"

"I'm not sure." Bob propped his chin on his hand as if relaxed, but Sophie saw his arm was trembling. "Gaby never talked about him."

"I guess he left her pregnant and without any support." Her throat ached with an old anger. "How could anyone be so cruel?"

Bob cleared his throat. "Times were a little different then. Men complained about being trapped and women felt ashamed if they got pregnant without marriage. A war between the sexes they called it. It was a different world. A much less forgiving one."

"It's not very forgiving now, if you ask me." Sophie sipped her tea, welcoming the hot liquid on her parched throat. "Being divorced. Sometimes I feel judged." Before Bob could reply, she asked, "Did you ever marry?"

"No, I didn't . . . have that opportunity."

"I find that hard to believe!" Sophie leaned toward him. "I'm sorry. Did something happen? You don't have to talk about it if you don't want to."

Bob looked down and rubbed a spot on the table. When he looked up, his eyes shone behind his glasses. "I have a hunch you know what I'm going to say." He paused. "There never was anyone who could compare to your mother. Not for me."

"But . . ." Sophie's voice wobbled. She didn't understand why she had never gotten to know Bob growing up if he and her mother were so close. Especially since they were family too, even if somewhat removed. "Why didn't you visit us when I was young?"

"I moved away right after you were born." Bob slid his glasses from his face. And I stayed away until about 1990, just in time to teach your friend Ronnie in the eighth grade."

"Not my friend. My husband, ex-husband I mean."

This warranted a sharp look. "No wonder the marriage didn't make it, if you weren't friends."

Hadn't Ronnie been her friend? Sophie thought so. But they had gone through that bad patch—and yet seeing him gave her hope, too. For a moment she felt bewildered, then she shook her head impatiently. "But how could you leave Mother behind if you cared so much for her?"

"I couldn't live here anymore. Not the way things were with Gaby." His neck bent forward until his chest collapsed a bit. Sophie could see the beginnings of a potbelly protruding.

Impulsively, she grasped his hand that lay on the table. "It would have been so wonderful to have you around. I'm sure she was at her best with you!" She felt heat rush to her face. What was she saying? She didn't know this man. He must think she was desperate for the first man who might have acted as a father to her. Sophie pushed her chair back. "I'd better go. I'm so sorry to have taken up so much of your time."

Bob lifted his hand and looked at it after hers slid away. "Don't go. I wasn't good enough for your mother, you have to know that."

"'Good enough.' To be what? A friend? A lover?"

"It was very complicated." His face drained of color as if she had punched him in the stomach.

Sophie knew she might have only one chance to know the truth. "You did know my father." And before she could think herself into silence, blurted: "Are you my father?"

To her confusion Bob stood up with such force his chair fell over behind him. "I wish I were."

Sophie wasn't convinced, but Bob's face had a stony, cornered cast. He looked poised to run. She feared if he retreated into the back of his shop, she would never see him again.

She poured more tea into each of their cups. Relieved when Bob edged back to the table, she said, "Mother told me my father went into the army after the Vietnam War. I don't know if he ever came back."

Bob cleared his throat and righted his chair. He sat back down. "He did, but not back to Smithfield."

"You do know him."

Bob fiddled with the milk pitcher. "He was my brother."

A yawning gap grew between Sophie and the rest of the room, as if she were looking at Bob through wavy glass.

"He died a long time ago—twenty years back. Cancer."

"Did my mother know that?"

"Oh, yes." Bob gave her a sad smile. "I called her. Told her James wanted to see her. But she was too angry."

Sophie felt angry herself. It seemed as if her own history had been kept from her.

Bob got up and went back to the case under the globe lamp. When he returned, he pushed a locket across the table. Sophie opened it up to see two miniature pictures inside. One was her mother. The other was a young man who had Bob's eyes.

"You can keep that," Bob said.

"Why didn't anyone tell me? Why did your brother never come to see me?" Sophie shut the locket so that it clicked and pressed it into her palm as if to pulverize it. The oval stayed intact, cool in her hand.

"I don't know anything," Bob said. "I asked Gaby to marry me after James died. I was living in Oregon then, but I would've come back. Anything for Gaby."

"How lucky she was." Sophie's voice was dull.

"Maybe that was it. For so much of her life she'd been so fortunate. Beautiful, smart, talented. Then life didn't turn out the way she wanted. So second best just wasn't good enough." Bob's face looked pinched.

Instead of arguing with him, Sophie sighed. "I always felt I was a second-best daughter to her too. She wanted a daughter more like herself." Sophie swiped at the tears she had been determined to keep at bay.

"But there was no one like her," Bob whispered.

The two stared at each other then, Bob holding out a clean, ironed handkerchief, Sophie letting the tears leak down her face. "No," she said. "There wasn't anyone like her."

"You're special too, you know," he said, pressing the handkerchief against her cheeks very gently. "You'll realize that someday."

Sophie's heart ached. She was afraid to tell Bob how much his words meant to her. What if he turned away? "I'm afraid I don't know how to be with another person. What if . . ." She stopped, not able to say—*what if I'm always going to be alone?* The word *alone* reverberated in her head.

"I know how you feel." He nodded as if she had voiced her greatest fear. "I've been scared all my life."

"I just meant—" Sophie began, but just at that moment, the tiny boy with the trumpet erupted from the clock and a large gong struck one. Another clock made an off-key chirp and two more in the back room chimed. The lights in the window began to dim.

"You'll come back again, won't you?" Bob asked.

The room darkened. She realized he wasn't sitting across from her anymore. His voice was distant, fading. "Just follow the light to the door."

At that, a thin line of blue light rippled along the scarred wood floor. She got up hastily, afraid she would be left sitting in the dark.

"Bob? Thank you," she called into the empty room as she stood at the door, her hand on the knob.

She wondered if he had heard her. She listened for a moment. "Goodbye. For now."

There was a soft sigh as if the room exhaled when she drew the door shut behind her and went out onto the street. The storefront was completely dark. It had that neglected look a place took on that had been vacant a long time.

Uncertainly, Sophie stood on the dark, deserted street. She looked down at her right hand—she was still clutching the locket Bob had given her—just as a maroon sedan pulled up to the curb. Ronnie sat behind the wheel.

As she stood there, she thought she heard the tinkle of a chime behind her from inside the shop. An urgent need to see the inside of the locket again seized her, and to show it to Ronnie. She straightened her shoulders and reached for the car door handle.

Noir by Night

Mean streets. Rain-lashed streets. Streets streaked by shadow. Empty streets stretching block after block. Streets with blown-out windows and rusted cars at the curb. Winding streets with lawns so green they're neon. I've prowled them all.

Around the next corner, a lone walker, tall and lean. Hat pulled down, collar pulled up, hands jammed in pockets. A man? A woman?

The head tilts up. Cheekbones that can cut wire. Huge brown eyes, a smooth brow. She pulls even with me. Her voice is husky: "Sarah."

"Julia." Of course. No one else walks like that, easy striding in her man-tailored slacks. She takes off her fedora, an affectation I once thought. Glossy brunette hair tumbles around her shoulders. The hat is not for display. It's a necessity. Without it, there's nowhere to hide.

"I've been looking for you," Julia says. She takes my arm and we walk on together. A cold wind whistles down the avenue. We lean into it together, two sharp angles advancing over the broad plain of the pavement.

"Yes, me too, for you. Where have you been?" I pull her closer.

"In Denver. My car broke down in the snow and I couldn't get back."

"Why didn't you call? I would've come to get you."

"Would you? Even in the middle of a case?" She shivers, tugs at her collar, jams the hat back on her head. "It's not any warmer here."

The twilight fades to black. It's November, the cold deepening. A few feet ahead of us, a bar beckons with neon. "Let's get a drink," I say.

We turn in to a small club on Central. Bottles line up in front of the mirror in rows—liquid comfort. The bar is clean and warm. Julia sits at the back table in the corner, and I go up to the counter, slide onto a stool. Jimmy comes over, sleeves rolled up to show off his muscles. "It's been too long," he says.

"I missed you too."

He winks at me. "What'll you have?"

"Johnnie Walker Black. Two. One with ice. Doubles."

He whisks out the bottle and glasses, gives us a hefty pour. "You're working the Dougherty case, right?"

"Right."

He puts his lips to my ear, breath whispering against my skin. "The old man died this morning. Word is, your girlfriend took him out." He runs a hand through his blond hair as he tips his head toward Julia.

"I don't think so," I say.

The mirror behind him is wavy. As I look into it, Julia's face blurs. Jimmy leans forward on his elbows. "You might have to prove that."

"She wasn't in town." I pluck an olive from a bowl on the bar, decide how much to tell him. "It wasn't a gun," I say.

"I know." He puts both hands out as if holding a taut rope and twists them in a downward motion. He grimaces to make his case.

I nod. "A wire, maybe a cord. Broke the hyoid bone. Someone quick and clean and strong."

"Still could be a woman."

"Not that woman." I pick up the two drinks. "Run a tab, Jimmy."

He nods. "Don't get in too deep, Sarah."

It's too late for that as Jimmy well knows. Someone as smart and beautiful as Julia didn't come around very often. Plus, she can handle a gun, wrestle a big man to the ground. She looks easy but proves to be tough, not, however, tough as nails. Who wants nails in their bed? No, Julia is tough like my cat Chloe, switching from a purr to a growl in a second.

We had started Premier Investigations two years ago. An ex-cop, Julia knows who to call—at the *Gazette*, at the downtown precinct, at the morgue. We had met when I was on a case and she was still on the force. Both of us saw more freedom in joining together.

At the table, I slide Julia her drink and sit down. We sip, eyeing each other. "I'm glad you're back."

She touches my glass with hers, smiles. As she drinks she asks, "Does Jimmy know anything about Dougherty?"

"He knows too much," I whisper. Only the investigating officers knew the means of death. "It's the old question: what does he know and when did he know it?"

"How do we get him?" Julia slides her hair behind her ear.

"He's vain. He can't resist boasting. And, he's always fancied you."

Julia nods. She flexes one hand on the table, her fingers long and supple, graceful like a cat's. "So, the usual? Bring him home on a promise and wrangle a confession? Just like in the movies?" Her even white teeth glow.

"The same. You're a star, Julia. I'll go to our place and wait. Give me a half hour. He'll turn the bar over to his pal George."

I wriggle out of my seat and stand, finishing the drink in one gulp. Waving to Jimmy, I exit the bar and head south of downtown. The street is quiet, in a sleepy neighborhood near a large park. I go in the back of our house, turning on just one dim light in the hall. Chloe meets me in the kitchen, twining around my ankles for food.

"Hi Punk. We've got a job tonight so let's eat up." Chloe makes a cooing noise as I open a can of tuna and put half of it in her bowl. She's a calico and fierce much of the time, a real pushover once a day when she gets her wet food. The mellow only lasts about ten minutes, though, and only toward her people who feed her.

I go into our bedroom and step into the closet, my .38 at the ready. Chloe jumps up on the chest of drawers, hunkers down.

Steps sound outside the house. I give Chloe the sign for quiet.

"You're such a doll." Jimmy giggles as Julia lets him in.

"Whiskey?" she asks.

"Sure."

I hear his coat as it lands on the living room sofa, then the pour. Ice cubes rattle. I can hear Jimmy's rapid breathing.

"No, in here," Julia says, leading him to our bedroom. I know she's put something in his glass to slow him down.

"Drink up big fella," Julia says. I hear buttons pop as she takes off his shirt.

"It's awfully dark in here," he says.

"Tell me again how you did Dougherty."

A groggy laugh. "How do you know I had anything to do with that?"

"It's your patch, sonny. And we know no one else is smart enough."

He giggles as she pushes him down on the bed.

"Give me a kiss, baby," he begs. "The old man had it coming. You know he did. Plus, there was all that cash in his place. I'll share with you."

"I'll bet you will."

Julia flicks on the light and the room explodes: Chloe launches herself off from the bureau onto his face, claws out like knives as she sails, as I come out of the closet with my gun.

"Sorry, Jimmy. It couldn't happen to a nicer guy." I hold up my mini recorder as Jimmy tries to dislodge Chloe, who is digging into his scalp.

"Get this fucking cat off my head!"

I think he'll tell us anything we want to hear. We tie Jimmy up and call our pal at the station to come and get him. In a few minutes, it'll all be over. And all without firing a shot. Who needs bullets when you have a secret weapon?

Chloe licks one paw, the right front one with the orange tip. "This is one pussycat you can't fox, Jimmy," Julia says with a wily smile.

The streets just got a little less mean. Just for tonight at least.

Everyday Monsters

In your freshman year your college mentor opens his office door after class for a routine conference with you. You follow him inside, happy to spend time as you often do—discussing the readings from class, his work in progress, or your latest essay, or reflecting on other subjects in the world of ideas. But on this day, Dr. W. closes the door. A former minister, he has good posture and is built like a fullback.

As you put down your notebook and books on his desk, Dr. W. launches himself at you. His weight, at least two hundred pounds, knocks you both to the floor. The knot of his tie pokes your cheekbone. He sounds excited and speaks rapidly, "I . . . I want . . ."

Has he said your name? You barely understand anything he says, only the heavy solid slab of his body pressing down on you.

You can't think, but as an active person you instinctively move. "No, I don't want . . . that!" Your voice hoarse, you push beyond your strength and manage to slide your one-hundred-thirty-five-pound self out from under his bulk and race for the door. "I trusted you!" you hope you call out as you fling yourself out the door.

You lose more than trust that day. Your belief in fairness abandons you. You feel like a prey animal.

Soon after, shaking, you cry in the office of your professor in another department, a very small woman with an outsize presence and a low seductive voice. It is 1969, you can't go to your dean. The words *sexual harassment* haven't yet entered everyday conversation. On this day, Dr. C. comforts and commiserates with you. You discuss strategy. Dr. C. spends a lot of time with you, railing against men like Dr. W.—she despises them as perpetrators, they exploit the very people they should protect she declares. When you leave her office, somewhat buoyed up, you vow never to allow Dr. W. an opportunity to be alone with you again.

Three years later, Dr. C., instead of driving you home after an evening of drinks and marvelous talk, takes you to her house, plugs in her car—it was the depths of winter in the northern Midwest—and leads you inside. To your confused, drunken surprise, Dr. C.'s shapely downturned lips loom close as she moves to kiss you. Panicked, you blurt out that you don't feel well and need to lie down. The prospect of a sick undergraduate in her home dampens Dr. C.'s. enthusiasm—she shows you the guest room and withdraws. The next morning, she drives you back to your apartment.

You and Dr. C. pretend that the evening never happened. You've worshiped Dr. C. for years and have chosen her as a model for how to be a professional and a woman in the world. The most upsetting thing for you is that you are attracted to Dr. C. and have been for a long time, but you can't imagine being intimate with your professor and idol. The idea terrifies you. You wish you could say to Dr. C.: "We have to talk about this," or sometimes, "Help. I'm so confused." You lose faith in your judgment of people that day.

That same year, you rent a house with two other friends, a man and a woman who share a room. The couple sleep in the downstairs bedroom, you in the upstairs one. At four in the morning after a night of drinking you stumble up the stairs, fling your clothes onto a chair, and climb into your bed. Instantly, you pass out. The glowing numerals of the clock greet you at 4:40 a.m. when your eyes pop open as burly arms clamp around you. Suddenly, you are excruciatingly sober. A male body, fully clothed, spoons your back side. The arms, the body, the slightly stale smell— nothing is familiar. Afraid of what you'll find, you resist turning your head. The seconds tick on and eventually, trapped, you force yourself to see who those thick arms belong to. You rotate your head on its pillow very slowly, and finally see in the dim light that the young man has dark hair and a messy bandage around his head. His black shoes, the laces untied, dangle at the foot of the bed.

"I used to know a girl who lived here," he mumbles.

"Oh." You automatically try to distract him. "She doesn't live here anymore. Um, what happened to your head?"

"Someone crashed a bottle on it. I just came from the ER."

As you struggle to think of what to ask him about the person who lived in this room before you, he says, wonder in his voice: "You don't have any clothes on, do you?"

The words galvanize you; you know you can't stay in this bed a second longer. "Hang on," you toss off. "I have to pee."

He loosens his arms. In seconds you leap up, grab a robe, and rush downstairs to wake your two housemates. The three of you huddle together on the sofa until the dark-haired young man stumbles down the steps, waves, and slumps out of the house. You call the police and stammer out what has happened. They bring the man back to apologize two days later. You gain some faith in the persistence of the police that day, but the stranger robs you of the sense that your home might be a safe place.

That same year you win an election for the head of student government at your college. You run the Board of Governors, a group of students who control every aspect of student affairs at the university with a fairly large budget. You gain confidence. On the day that you have to visit your former chairperson to sign a form to switch majors, the woman, Dr. H., does not offer you a chair. You kneel beside her desk and sign.

"I never thought I'd see you on your knees!" Dr. H.'s voice, waspish and triumphant, pierces your ears.

You glance up at this successful woman, at least forty years older than you are. A nauseous feeling spreads throughout your abdomen. You want to strike back at the woman. All you can think of to say as you stand, towering over Dr. H, is "How interesting that *you* should say that." On this day you lose respect for women who bully other women.

In 1974 you finish your MA degree and decide to take two years off before going back to graduate school. In your first administrative job at a major university your boss cozies up to you at the copy machine. He has a shiny forehead. "I dreamed about you last night." He scans the length of your body. You blush furiously and turn away. Did you respond with a nervous laugh? You fear you might have. Looking back, you wish you had had the presence of mind to say: "Your dreams are about you, not me. Please keep them to yourself." You vow to learn how to assert yourself.

Over the years, episodes of what you think of as betrayal continue but they change shape: there are the two erstwhile allies in your department who don't support your promotion to full professor; the colleague who mystifyingly turns to you at lunch to say with others listening: "It's a mystery that you and I didn't run away to Mexico when we had a chance"; the powerful professor who asks you to lunch to discuss your career but who, once there, declares that he intends to dismantle the PhD program you head, the one with the best graduate students in the department. These encounters leave you reeling, the ground fracturing under your feet even as you stagger to find a place to stand.

Over time, you learn from these opportunities. You practice your political skills, going to town halls with students in protest, standing up at meetings to argue for younger colleagues. You try not to be a person who complains and fumes but rather one who presses for change. One day in the mail room you copy an essay by a famous feminist and gender scholar who quits her university in protest, fatigued from fighting the tightly knit institutional club that excludes outsiders, many women, some men, others of color. A colleague, not an ally, asks about the article. "Aren't you glad that could never happen here?" he asks. You ask him if he is kidding. He smiles and waves.

You survive attempts to sabotage you and your career. You write a story about Ivory Power, the codes of conduct and connections that are every bit as guarded as the keys to the childhood tree house or the rules that governed the elite society of Old New York in the nineteenth century. You vow to keep your sense of humor and claim laughter, friendship, and community as weapons of joy and resistance.

Rather than have your program diminished through slow strangulation, you enlist help from your dean and others to change departments, gaining promotion to full professor as well as supportive colleagues. You champion your male and female graduate students and younger colleagues, tutoring them in strategies to ward off being torpedoed by snarky professors who do not want them to succeed.

In middle age you realize that you've spent decades in teaching paying back the many gifts you've received from the insights and generosity of your great teachers early in your life and your many wonderful students who've shared their minds and hearts with you.

You know that every path has its price and that every pilgrimage offers the potential for gaining strength and courage. Sometimes your journey seems like a complicated and byzantine bargain, at others like unearthing the provenance of a painting left in a contested will.

Years later you snowshoe to a saddle at the top of the Sandia Mountains with your wife. The day is clear and bright. The city of Albuquerque spreads out below the mountain range to the cottonwood forest along the Rio Grande and beyond. The vista reminds you how at night you can see the stunning beauty of the city from the houses in the foothills, the darkness everywhere punctured by bright lights.

"Sometimes your greatest purpose is to be a tiny light in a dark place," you recall a spiritual teacher telling you.

You turn your back on the view. Your body warm from the effort of the upward climb in the cold dry air, you exchange a contented smile with your wife as you begin to trek down the mountain.

Regret

At nine o'clock on a windy autumn night, I walked down Lomas and passed the coffee shop at Second. The place looked closed up, dark, a little spooky. But then I saw the neon "Open" sign blink on. Through the street-side window I spotted a thin figure shuffling around the dim interior. I waited a minute and went in. Harry stood there behind the counter, one shoulder hitched higher than the other.

~

I had been looking for him for five years. Not continuously. Just so you know, Harry and I started a business back in '08. Hardware, yard tools, and a few other things you might want when you dash out in the middle of a project to grab new needle-nose pliers, a roof shingle or two—like a cold beer, some Fritos, peanuts, that sort of thing. And coffee. Harry believed that coffee was more than an essential food group. More like water. Or blood. So, coffee brewed at a steady clip in our shop, sometimes three kinds, poured into big thermos servers. With a new batch ready to serve at the flip of a switch.

Pretty soon we had to put chairs and a few little tables in the store because Fred would slouch on in and see Duke, and they'd need to talk. Or the roofer who was supposed to be working on Dan's house jawed with Harry instead. Over coffee, naturally.

When our business went belly-up after three years, it wasn't exactly a surprise that Harry started the coffee shop a couple of years later. Coffee made us go broke in the first place. People forgot about their nails and caulking guns and fence posts and just kicked back. You don't make a lot of money this way, with people buying one cup of coffee and sitting around for two hours. Long enough that they forgot what they had come in to buy and left empty-handed, happy to have spent time chewing over the local gossip with their pals.

"Hell, Harry, ditch the goddamn coffee," I said about once a month. "Let's get serious and sell something."

"I am serious, Junior. A good cup of coffee helps these guys figure out what they need."

My name is Ed, but I'm three years younger than Harry. He started calling me that in high school. I didn't much like it, but thank God it didn't catch on in town with anyone else. "Well, then, maybe they just don't need what we have for sale," I would say, my temper beginning to simmer. "The books don't lie. The inventory isn't going anywhere."

"Shit." Harry crossed his ropy forearms. "Not our fault. These yahoos don't know how to build anything. That's the problem."

That pretty much sums up year two. By year three, my marriage teetered on the edge of going bust, we fell two months behind on our mortgage, and I struggled through the nights moonlighting as a bartender at the edge of town.

"I've got to call it quits, Harry," I said one frosty November day. I remember it well because the pipes in my kitchen clogged up and putrid water puddled in both sinks. My wife, Maggie, threw up her hands.

"I don't suppose you can fix this," she said.

"Ha, I know you're going to make a crack about the shoemaker's children or—"

"Ed, it's time for a change around here. I'm teaching at a high school short on staff, and you're working all hours at the bar. And you know what? We're not supporting each other—we're keeping the hardware store afloat."

She had a point. "Okay." I gave in easy that time. That very day I went into the store—"Fixtures" we called it. Stupid name, Harry's idea—and I told Harry: "I'm done. When you sell all this stuff—" (what was I saying, nothing had sold for years!) "—you can send me a check."

"Quitter." Harry said, taking a step toward me, his arms stiff at his sides. "Sad sack." Then he threw in for good measure: "Pessimist."

"Thank you, Harry." We didn't shake hands.

That night I lay in bed next to Maggie, gnawing on a cookie. She hated the crumbs on the sheets, but my blood sugar had cratered. I thought of Harry standing alone in the store as I left, flanked by boxes and ladders and racks of electric heaters like silent soldiers. "Do acceptance and regret always go together?" I asked.

Maggie didn't answer. She had already fallen asleep.

~

I didn't see Harry for a long time after that. Maggie and I had a lot of catching up to do, with each other, with our sagging bank balance. I took another job working in the library—no coffee allowed; it was kind of a relief. Maggie kept on teaching. Finally, we caught up enough that she started classes in a graduate program; she decided she wanted to become a school counselor.

It took some time, I can tell you, before I scrubbed the smell of failure off my skin from the hardware store. Every cent I had put into it was a total loss. Maybe Harry sold some of the inventory, but he didn't share it with me. And I didn't ask. I had some pride after all.

On my thirty-fifth birthday, Maggie took me out to dinner at a steak place we liked called "Lucky's Finest." It was kind of a joke between us, you know, a throwback kind of place—it looked like the '60s with its red booths, lots of mirrors on the wall and a big shiny bar with exotic brews on tap. The bartender had a high wattage smile and a wink for the ladies. But the restaurant had grass-fed beef and real hand-cut fries, plus salads with Maggie's favorite, arugula and goat cheese.

Maggie looked good. She had that honey-colored skin that took a dynamite tan. She had lost a few pounds; her skin-tight jeans fit just right.

"Okay, truth." Maggie said, refolding her napkin and leaning forward. "You're thirty-five. So . . ."

"So?" I said.

"You have a college degree, Ed, and you've been running from committing yourself to any career path the whole time I've known you."

"*Career path?*" I repeated. "Whoa. Maybe I should have voted no on graduate school for you." I sighed. She was right, of course. I did have a degree, in history. "Look, I use my degree all the time—I read everything I can. It's why I love being in the library."

"Then go and get a degree in library science. Or something."

I couldn't help it, I felt rejected. Wasn't I paying my share of the bills? "So, are you embarrassed?" I asked Maggie. "To be married to a low achiever or something? Kind of like the kids you're going to be counseling. Or maybe I should say you'll be counseling them so they won't be like me."

"Stop right there." She raised a hand. "It's just that ever since the hardware store closed you've kind of been moping around."

"Shit," I said. "You know my dad was such a booster for having your own business. 'Ed, stop reading and sell something' he'd say twice a day."

"Okay, you tried business." Maggie spoke in a very reasonable tone. You couldn't argue with it, ever. "Can you say you liked it?"

"God no!" I surprised myself by how angry I felt. It felt good so I said "Hell no!" even louder. I felt the big weight of my dad's hand lift from between my eyes.

"I love you just the way you are," Maggie said. "But I don't like to see you feeling washed-up just because one thing you tried didn't work out."

I ate my last fry, which by this time was soggy.

~

"I don't suppose you just want a cuppa joe." A single bright bulb hung by a cable over the counter, pooling light around Harry's still form. His sparse hair glittered. He turned to me, his right eyelid drooping from a long-ago encounter with a barbed-wire fence.

I slid onto a barstool in front of the counter. "A little more than that."

Harry stared at the beam above his head as if counting to ten to keep his temper in line. "We're square, Junior. How about leaving the past in the fucking past?"

He didn't sound hopeful, but not morose either. Just flat. Just Harry. "That's fine with me. Except for the money." I sucked in a breath. "I want to go back to school, and things are a little tight."

I pulled a folded sheet of paper out of my pocket and laid it on the counter. "Twenty thousand. A lowball estimate on what we put into the store. In fact, I gave myself a haircut. As you know, I put that much down toward the renovation on that building when we leased it. I'm not even asking for the fifteen thousand I spent on stocking the store. If I recall, you put in ten. The rest, all the overtime hours both you and I put in"—here I had to put a clamp on it not to roll my eyes—"what you used to call our 'sweat equity,' we'll call that a wash."

I noticed the prominence of Harry's Adam's apple in his skinny neck as he swallowed. "Generous," he said. "I suppose you think you're a generous son of a bitch." He kept his tone even, but his forehead gleamed with sweat.

The paper I had given him trembled in his hand. I had been so focused on making my case to Harry that I had missed the obvious fact that his rangy frame had shrunk to downright stringy. "You okay, Harry?"

He just grunted. "I don't have twenty thousand," he said after a while. "You got your wife and your house. All I got? What I don't got."

Jesus. Harry could always make me feel guilty for being alive. But I had come this far. "Look, can we work out something?"

"Like an installment plan?" A ghost of a smile played over Harry's pale face. "Remember when we bought those refrigerators that way? Hell, the profit on those barely covered the damn service fee."

Was it hot in the shop? Sweat began to ooze between my shoulder blades. "Whatever you can do. I'm serious. I need the money."

"We all need something, Junior. I'd almost forgotten that, until I saw you."

I ducked my head. What did that mean? I tapped my index fingers on the bar, keeping time to a slow tune my mom had liked to sing. "Summertime." The song calmed me down whenever I thought about it. "Well, Maggie's waiting for me. I guess we'll talk again. I'm glad you finally got your coffee shop." I turned away from Harry for a few seconds and took a closer look. Cobwebs traced the corners of the ceiling like cracks on an old china cup.

Harry planted his hands on the counter and leaned forward, his neck jutting forward at a painful angle. The sweat on his forehead looked about to drip. "I just don't have it," he said.

My face flushed. Harry looked just plain sick and that was the truth. I didn't need to see the rows of pill bottles on his nightstand to wonder how long he had in this world. I backed away from the counter. "Hey, man, sorry to bother you." I headed for the door.

When I left the building and started up the street I turned back and saw that the "Open" sign on the shop had blinked off. I remembered I had left the sheet of paper with the hardware accounting on the bar. Ashamed after seeing Harry in such bad shape, his shoulders hunched with pain, I wished I had ripped the damn thing up. Accounting just kept track of money. Something you had sometimes and other times you didn't.

I remembered the Harry I knew when we started the hardware store: tough, gutsy, energy to burn. Things you can't buy.

Or bargain for.

EXHIBIT D

Old Vines

Marlene opened the door to the restaurant. She had spent the last five minutes peering through the beveled glass, wondering if the person she was supposed to meet had arrived yet. The place appeared to be half full of people who looked younger than she was. She resisted tracing her finger through the thin skim of fog her breath had made on the glass. *This is dumb*, she told herself. She sucked in a deep breath and walked in.

Her entrance coincided with a din as a waiter with a full tray skidded on something—oil? Spilled wine?—and went down on one knee. Everyone stopped talking. Thirty faces turned toward Marlene, who stood just to the right of the waiter. Her face burned. She shrank over to the coatrack on the far wall by the restroom and removed her heavy wool coat as the waiter—the tray teetering, the dishes clattering—managed to hold steady, get back on his feet, and take a step forward. Several guests cheered. Marlene turned her face toward the coats and scarves thrown onto pegs along the wall.

She hadn't felt like going out this evening. Why hadn't she listened to that niggling warning creeping over her scalp, always a preface to a headache? She wanted to grab her coat and run.

The room had settled back down, the humming of conversation ramped up once again. The heroic waiter had finished serving the table of four. "Awesome catch!" a young man with floppy brown hair said to the blond waiter. "You a gymnast?" asked his partner, her eyes taking in the waiter's strong slender build.

This is not my kind of place, Marlene chanted to herself, slinking over to the hostess station. "Um, my name is Marlene Stratton. I'm not sure my dinner companion is here. Derrick. Derrick Wilson."

She wondered if the name was a false one. Who was named "Derrick" anymore? Who had ever been? She realized that by going on this blind date she was gambling. She never gambled.

The hostess did not seem perturbed. She flashed a big smile at Marlene. "There is a reservation. For two," she said as if everything were just fine.

Which it was not! Marlene had let herself be talked into this date, encounter, meeting, whatever the hell you would call it, by her best friend Rachel. "Derrick is a doll. Supersmart. And funny . . ." Rachel had clutched her stomach as if remembering some hilarious gale of laughter.

"Would you like to be seated?" The hostess asked, a thin furrow appearing between her wide eyes.

"Ah, yes, that would be nice." Marlene wished for only one thing—a drink, yes, that would sort everything out. Maybe two drinks. God, what if Derrick didn't drink? Well, she didn't care if he did or didn't. Here she was, she didn't even know this person and already she was thinking she should conform to his tastes. No wonder she hated dating. No one used that word anymore, but Marlene didn't know what else to call it.

The hostess escorted her to the table next to the one where the waiter had almost disgorged his tray all over his four patrons. The two women were giggling, the men checking out the women's necklines. Marlene fought an urge to flee.

"And here's the wine list," her waiter said, handing her an oversize menu.

Before he could leave, Marlene said, "How about you bring me your favorite Zin that you have by the glass?"

"Of course. How about a glass of Cline Old Vines?"

Marlene nodded. She felt short of breath. It was all she could do not to demand, "Wine, immediately, please!" Instead, she managed, "Thank you." She wondered if she was developing a heart problem. Her chest ached with tension.

Mercifully, the wine arrived promptly. She was just raising the glass when the door to the restaurant opened and a tall, thin man with a neat moustache stepped inside. Marlene shrank. He looked like her high school French teacher more than twenty years ago.

She shielded her face with one hand and looked the other way, hoping the man would continue on. But in a moment, he cleared his throat and leaned over. "Um, Marlene?"

She removed her hand from her cheek. "Oh, yes, that's me. You must be Derrick."

He smiled, a sweet, shy smile. Marlene revised her opinion of him—he was not like her high school French teacher, who had been very demanding. Marlene thought of herself as reticent. Of course, in that case, they would be two shy people. What would they talk about?

"Sit down, please," she thought to say as Derrick still stood, his smile fading but still sweet.

Derrick sat across from her and began to struggle out of his long, heavy coat. As if by magic, a waitperson hurried over. "May I hang up your coat, sir?"

"Oh, thank you," Derrick looked relieved. "You know," he leaned over the table toward Marlene, "the last time I was in a restaurant with my coat lying across the chair someone spilled some kind of brown sauce all over it. It was embarrassing to put it back on."

"I'll bet," Marlene said, having a slug of wine. The coat story was kind of a conversation stopper. What now? "I got here a little early, so I ordered a glass of wine."

"Good idea," Derrick said. "I think I'll do the same." He studied the wine list. "They don't have a lot by the glass, do they?"

"This Clines Zin is really good."

"Okay." Derrick looked at her with pale-blue eyes. "I'm afraid I'm not very good at making decisions," he said.

"I'm not either!" Marlene said. The wine was beginning to warm her up a bit. She looked around. The restaurant had a trendy faux-factory look about it with high ceilings and brick walls. Lights hung from exposed pipes. But then the tables and chairs were a warm hardwood like maple, very comfortable, and each table had a candle that actually cast the kind of shadowed light that all the magazines told you was most flattering after forty. Marlene was forty-two.

The waiter returned, took Derrick's wine order, and withdrew. "So, how do you know Rachel?" Marlene asked, exhausting the one subject she knew they had in common.

"Rachel's mom and mine are best friends," he said. "They go way back. I think maybe to elementary school."

"Really?" Marlene thought about Mrs. Knobloch, Rachel's mom. She seemed elegant, at least her clothes were. And she always wore beautiful bracelets and earrings, silver usually, with turquoise or jade.

"Rachel's been my best friend since high school," Marlene confided. She took a risk: "She and I are kind of opposites. You know, Rachel is so outgoing, always knows something clever to say. . . ."

"She does!" Derrick exclaimed. "She's like her mom that way." The two of them looked at each other. Marlene had an urge to giggle. She liked how Derrick was modest and easy, like he had nothing to prove. He had a good haircut too, his fine sandy hair complementing his angular face.

"So, tell me about yourself," Derrick said.

"Not fair—that's what I was going to say!" Marlene said. At that moment, Derrick's wine arrived and in no time at all they were clinking glasses.

"I hate small talk," Derrick said quietly. "So, I was serious, tell me about yourself." His light-blue eyes looked receptive.

Marlene sipped her wine. "Well, I'm switching careers," she said.

"Okay." Derrick waited for her to continue.

"I just decided!" Marlene said and laughed. "You're such a good listener, or at least you seem to be. I've always wanted to be a therapist, and I don't know . . . there's something about you, you make me see that listening is just the most *important* thing. I just realized I've had it with middle management." She made a face. "At a brokerage company."

Derrick nodded solemnly. "Soulless," he said.

"How did you know?" Marlene signaled the waiter. When he arrived, she ordered a bottle of the Zinfandel.

"My mom is a stockbroker. Sometimes I feel like a statistic, you know?"

"Exactly," Marlene said.

They shared a satisfied smile as if having decided something momentous. Just as Marlene's glow began to fade a bit—was this subject, their only subject besides Rachel, now closed?—fortunately, their waiter arrived with their bottle of wine and to take their order.

Having ordered a Caesar salad and the chef's special sea scallops (Derrick ordered the same), Marlene cast about for what to say when she heard a high-testosterone laugh from a table off to the side of them. Two men had been sitting there for some time and now there was a third, standing and weaving slightly, at the table. "Hey dude, that's my chair—want to fight me for it?"

One of the men seated, late thirties Marlene thought, spread his legs wider and folded his arms. "Look, fella, I think you have the wrong table. My friend Larry and I are having a quiet drink, so . . ."

". . . so you're like, together?" the weaving man said. He pulled himself up straight. "Well, sorreee, hate to break up a budding romance."

The other man, Larry, cocked his head at his friend, one eyebrow lifted. Marlene admired people who could pull that off. He was George Clooneyhandsome, too. Then he pushed his chair back and stood—all six foot five muscled inches of him.

But to Marlene's surprise, he spoke quietly. "Come on, Dave, let's just let him have the table." The two men moved to another table nearer the bar, leaving Mr. Weaving and Aggressive by himself.

The hero waiter with the overloaded tray earlier rushed over to him. "Look, sir, you'll have to keep your voice down . . ."

"Fine," the guy snarled and went to the end of the bar. He tumbled his bulk into a chair. He raised one finger and the bartender slid a pint toward him. The bartender also raised one finger and said something, warning him that this was his last drink; Marlene registered his no-arguments tone.

Derrick leaned toward Marlene. "Wow. Larry could have wiped the walls with that guy."

"You know him?" Marlene asked, referring to the familiar way he said *Larry.*

"No, just eavesdropping." Derrick flushed a bit. "Good for them for not getting into it."

"I don't know them either," Marlene said. "Dave and Larry have some restraint. How unusual." They caught each other's eyes and smiled.

"So," Derrick said, sounding more relaxed. "You're getting out of the brokerage business? After how long?"

"Um, sixteen years total, but ten with this company." Marlene broke off a crust of bread from the plate that their waiter had just deposited and dipped it into olive oil.

Derrick nodded. "You've had a long career already." He considered, his hand drifting over to the bread plate. He picked up a small end piece. "When you say you want to be a therapist, did you take some of those courses in college? Or maybe you're doing that now?" Derrick really had the most amazing light-blue eyes, almost like turquoise. Marlene was so unused to men listening to her—the men at the brokerage company barked into their phones all day long and occasionally at her—that she hesitated before replying.

"I was a double major. Psychology and finance. My parents are both lawyers, so they weren't so encouraging about the psychology part."

Was that true, Marlene wondered? Her parents had always been so supportive—she was an only child—but, still, instead of going to graduate school in psychology she had taken a job. "It wasn't really their fault," she said aloud. "I think I needed to be independent, to go to work, and then I got offered a job right away with a large company. In Los Angeles. It seemed like an adventure at the time."

They sipped their wine for a moment. Marlene noticed Mr. Aggressive was still hunched over his glass. He didn't seem to be drinking. Was he even awake? She turned back to her companion. "What about you? I think Rachel told me you you're a professor."

Derrick shifted in his chair. "Associate professor. At Northwestern. Biology. It's okay, but I'm not sure I'd go into higher education now. The funding thing in the sciences is so crazy. I spend most of my time applying for grants. But I guess I'm lucky to have a tenured position." He looked unhappy when he said that, and Marlene wanted to know more, but just then Mr. Weaving and Aggressive at the end of the bar had come back to their part of the restaurant, making his way now to the new table where the two men had settled themselves.

"Larry," he slurred, and winked at Dave. "I'm so sorry you had to move. So sorry."

Larry and Dave shifted their shoulders away from him.

"Hey, pay attention, 'm apologizing here." The drunk tipped his drink, a pint of something very dark, maybe Guinness, and spilled it into Larry's lap.

Larry leaped up like a cat and towered over Aggressive, who was laughing and trying to finish what was left of his beer at the same time. Larry grabbed the glass with one hand and slammed it down on the table. Beer slopped over the table and dripped onto the floor. With his other hand, he grabbed Aggressive's arm and pinned it up behind him. "I think you're done here, bud," Larry said.

By this time, Dave was also on his feet, and the waiter had returned with a towel in an agony of apology.

"Wait a minnit, I'm just talkin' to these fellas!" Aggressive said with a hyena-like giggle. Bent over, he winced in pain.

The three men dragged the drunk to the door and muscled him onto the street. There was a muffled sack-of-potatoes-falling sound.

"—or I'll call the police!" Marlene heard as the waiter came back in with the two others. "Thanks, guys," he said. "The next drink is on me. Dinner too if you want it." The three men put their heads together, laughed, and the waiter moved off.

"Well, this is exciting," Derrick said admiringly, watching Larry and Dave reseat themselves to cheers from other diners.

"I'll say," Marlene agreed. They raised their glasses and toasted Larry and Dave while the applause died down. Larry stood up gracefully and took a bow. He gestured at Dave, who put up his hands with a big grin, declining to stand.

The room settled down after that and their salads came.

"So much applause. It's like we're in a theater!" Derrick said, spearing a tomato.

Marlene nodded at this insight. "Have you ever noticed how most plays take place in just one room where the most amazing things happen?"

Derrick ate a forkful of greens. "True. And that's the case in your new career too, right? It's just the client and the therapist in that room but the outcome sometimes shakes the walls." He looked up, a tinge of crimson shading his neck.

Marlene considered. Was he embarrassed because he had been in therapy? "Do you like the theater?" she asked instead.

"Actually, I do." Derrick raised his wineglass. "I was in a few plays in college."

"An actor!" Marlene exclaimed. "I did that in high school. Somehow, I didn't pursue it, though."

"Me neither," Derrick said, leaning back in his chair. He looked at the ceiling. "Therapy and theater. Two sides of a coin."

Marlene giggled. "Or maybe the same side. Of a one-sided coin!" She was feeling comfortably tipsy. This was kind of fun. And Derrick's comment about therapy and theater was insightful. He looked conventional, but she was beginning to see something else there too. "Do you think you'll ever audition for a play again?" She asked him.

"I just might," he said, a defiant gleam in his eyes.

They didn't say anything for a minute; they both focused on finishing their salads. Derrick slid his plate off to the side. "So, that drunk who was in here. What do you think, does he need a stage or a therapist?"

Marlene smiled at Derrick, deciding that the evening definitely qualified as an eventful one. And they hadn't even received their main courses yet. "I wonder how many sessions I'd have to have with him to answer that."

She poured them each more wine, then sipped, her posture relaxing. The Zinfandel was very smooth. Old Vines. She liked the sound of that. For the first time she felt that she too was improving with age.

Flight

Vicky had one strategy—getting out of Dodge. As long as she left before the other person did, she could breathe. So, she left, she moved, she quit, she ran, she disappeared.

At three, she was placed in foster care. And again, two years later. And again . . . well, she didn't want to count the ways that her life went to hell over and over.

She looked around the room at the nine women in her support group. "But here's the thing." She took a deep breath. "I consider myself an optimist."

Silence from the group. Then one person, very hesitantly, smiled—a tiny smile, one corner of her mouth lifting.

To save the moment, Vicky started to laugh. Kind of a tinny, fake laugh, but it was the best she could do. "I do," she said. "After all, I'm here. Right now. I've been in this group for three years. It's the longest commitment I've ever made."

Brenda, the facilitator, spoke up after a long minute. "Thank you, Vicky. That's fantastic." She raised her arms like a bird about to take off, encouraging other responses.

"Yeah, Vicky, we're so glad you're here," Bridget piped up. Her head was shaved on one side; the other side sprouted a floppy platinum mane to her ears. Vicky knew she could never wear a hairstyle like that—her head had some bumps. But this woman was gorgeous, with flawless skin and one of those heart-shaped perfect faces that didn't need hair around it, or the right earrings, or makeup.

Murmurs and cheers burst out from the other eight people.

Brenda checked her phone. "It's time for a break," she said. Dutifully, the group got up and went to the table for Cokes or coffee. The coffee was a bit of a gamble, at times so dark and strong that a big pour of half-and-half barely cut the bitterness, at others so weak that you could see the bottom of the cup.

Vicky ducked out the side door. She found her car in the parking lot and leaned against it, her body trembling. Today she had to leave at the break. Especially after spilling her guts. Sometimes she felt she had a sign on her back and forehead that said *Freak*. She couldn't face anyone coming over to her, the sympathetic nods, the pats on the back, the "Hey, let's get together soon. I know just how you feel." That came from Colby. Either she had the worst life anyone had ever had in any century, or she masqueraded as a huge, quivering ball of empathy. But maybe she was genuine. Who knew?

Still shaky, Vicky aimed the car toward home. She drove like an old lady, someone told her once, really close to the steering wheel, peering at the road ahead. But she was only five two, and her legs especially were short, so she didn't really see what else she could do with her *driving position*. She could still hear the prim voice of the drivers ed person back in high school going on about that. She just hoped she wouldn't get in an accident because the airbag would probably kill her. Vicky imagined the bag blowing up, slamming into her chest or her face, fracturing bones, cutting off her breath.

She pulled over into a convenience mart. The light began to leak from the sky and her sunglasses were the only ones she had with her. She squinted into the gloom. "Okay, pull it together, come on, *come on*," she chanted. She bought a bottle of water in the small store, dumping the contents of her pocket on the counter.

"How's it goin'," the guy at the counter said without looking at her. Really built, he had huge, corded arms and a broad chest.

"Great, great. You?" Her voice had a croaky vibe. She thought she sounded like a junkie. She coughed a few times, trying to clear her throat. If only she still smoked or drank, she thought, she wouldn't be this spooked just talking to the store clerk. A drink, that's what she really needed. But that was the one line she couldn't afford to cross. Not this time.

"Hey, better take care of that cough," Mr. Muscle said. "Ya never know, it's the little things that get you." This time he aimed his eyes at her face, his eyebrows arching.

"Thanks. Yeah, good night." Vicky speed-walked out to the parking lot.

She opened her car door, twisted the cap off the bottle and gulped half the water. Her head had that light feeling. God, she needed to get home and eat something. Had she forgotten to eat lunch? It was past her dinner time, eight o'clock. Suddenly she was ravenous; she checked the glove box for a granola bar. Nothing. One stick of gum. She fumbled unwrapping it, tried to roll it up but it was stiff as a board. She gnawed on it anyway.

She should have stayed home. Between the group and Mr. Muscle—convenience store, what a joke. *Inconvenient*, or worse, *torture*, just like the support group. She slumped in her car. Okay, time to go, just three more miles.

A loud rap on her window. She froze. *Quick, lock the doors, fast.* Fast. She looked up. It was Mr. Muscle.

"Hey, lady, sorry to scare you." He grinned at her, a perfectly nice grin if you were in the mood.

Uncertain, she gnawed on her lip.

"You left a bill on the counter, that's all. Ten bucks. Here." He motioned for her to roll down her window. She did, just two inches though.

He threaded the ten through the opening and then backed away, hands out, empty. "Take it easy," he said, again with that big smile.

The ten fluttered into her lap. Vicky watched his easy glide toward the store.

She lowered her window. "Hey!" she called out. He turned around. She waved and cracked a small smile. "You too!" she said.

Vicky started the car and cautiously backed out, narrowly missing a post. That wasn't so hard, exchanging a few words with a stranger. A considerate stranger, of course, she had been lucky there. Maybe she should get to know a few folks in her apartment building. There were always things to talk about—the elevator not working, for instance. She heard her grandmother's voice suddenly: *The lift is on the fritz! Again!* That woman knew just who she was.

Two right turns and a left after two blocks—Vicky always took the same route wherever she went, one she had memorized. Just in case, she wrote it down on a sticky note and stuck it on the dashboard too.

She jerked to a stop one block from her place. A young woman stood on the corner in the near-dark, clutching a small girl's hand. Propped up against a suitcase was a sign, *Need help.*

Vicky knew those words in her bones. She inched the car forward, rolled down her window a few inches. "Hey, lady."

The woman lurched over to her.

"Here." Vicky handed her the ten Mr. Muscle had returned to her.

The woman's weary face lit up. She put her hand over her heart and bowed forward. "Thanks, oh thank you thank you . . ."

Her face flushing, Vicky nodded. "You take care," she said, wriggling her fingers at the little girl.

Vicky drove the last block and parked her car in the narrow space in front of her building. "It's the little things that get you," she recited, trying to mimic Mr. Muscle. But then she thought: *it's the little things that get you through, too.* Next time she stopped at that convenience mart she would let him know.

Dry Tinder

My mother was pretty and bright as a new-minted penny, my father always said when he spoke of meeting her for the first time. The nickname stuck. Radiating hope and vitality, Penny knew how to keep things alive. Without Mother's attention we would have shriveled like the plants in her garden after the first freeze.

At mealtime, our faces tipped toward her like new growth seeking light. I remember thinking: *We are all her creatures*. And how our attention gratified her. Her fair German skin flushed and warmed by our watching, her tall figure erect and firm, she set steaming platters in front of us. "Is everybody ready to eat?" she would ask.

"Starved," my father would answer on cue. She would pass the plates, her chameleon eyes flashing blue, other times gray or green, as we dispatched the mounds of baked buttercup squash shining with melted butter, the stacks of sliced rare roast, the bowls of Swiss chard and fresh peas. Like satellites adrift in our orbits, we gravitated around her solid, blazing center.

Mother yearned to satisfy us, to make us want to stay with her, and so she poured her robust spirit into us. Her immense energy astonished us all, until one summer it just wasn't there. In the end, she simply exhausted herself.

One day she came in from the garden and collapsed in the kitchen. A stroke. Her decline was short, her death unfussy.

The day before her funeral, humidity veiled the sky. The arrangements had all been made, neighbors had stocked the house with casseroles and goodwill, leaving me free to worry about seeing my sister after two years and what we might say to each other. I waited for Jenny on the front porch in the afternoon, hoping for a breeze to relieve the July heat.

My sister's dirty brown Jeep careened up the short hill from the main road and into the yard, tires skidding in a froth of gravel. A haze of dust sifted around her as she jumped out. Supple and bright-skinned, Jenny seemed untouched by gravity or time.

Jenny brushed her cheek against mine and then stepped back. "When I drive up that road, no matter what time of day or night, I know you're going to be sitting and waiting for me in that chair. I begin to anticipate it miles away. And the closer I get, the more I feel anxious about it. What if you're not there? And what if you are? By the time I come up over the hill and I see you, I'm terrified. And relieved."

A wave of annoyance washed over me. Why couldn't Jenny just say she was glad to see me? I hoped I could be patient through the familiar friction— the initial anticipation of seeing my sister, then the flare as the sparks flew into the dry tinder of our relationship. "What is that supposed to mean?"

She folded her arms across her chest and examined my face, as if looking for lines there she hadn't seen before. "You're a source of great wonder to me, Kath. That's all."

I had left my law practice in Minneapolis and moved home to help Mother manage the farm after my brother, David, died five years ago. By then my marriage had crumbled, and the farm challenged me in midlife to nurture the land that our family had homesteaded. I wish I had seen the place when my great-grandparents first came, the stark grandeur of the prairie, the grasses sweeping the sky, bent and golden, sun-cured, how the wind pushed at this northern world, sky and earth poised for its next breath.

Jenny claimed to be mystified that I had left the city to come back to North Dakota. The rolling fields soothed me but choked Jenny. There wasn't much I could say to counter her view that I had made a big mistake.

"This is just who I am," I said. "You make mysteries out of the commonplace."

"Is that so terrible? I longed for mystery when I lived here." Jenny waved a hand at the quiet farmyard, and I remembered how as a girl she would twirl around with her arms outstretched, her blond hair flying in the sun like a dazzling pinwheel pointing everywhere at once.

Prompted by the vigor of the young woman in front of me, my mind flashed back to the image of Mother lying in her bed the day before she died. Her strong-featured face had pulled away from her bones. Flesh had given way to folds of skin. Her nose and chin, raw ridges of bone, protruded from the soft tissue. Mystery. There was no mystery in what time and illness had done to Mother. The memory itself fatigued me. "I don't have to look for mystery."

Jenny looked away. "I'm sorry. About Mother. I can't imagine. How can this place still be here if she's not? I never supposed she could die while this was all still here . . ." She gestured at the blooming shrubs and flower beds, the multihued landscape Mother had built out of the prairie. Jenny bit her lip, her green eyes softening.

I went to her and put my arms around her. I felt her stiffen against me. Always this same resistance. Even when she was small her very skin seemed charged by a restless current. She stepped away, blinking back tears. "Kath, there's nothing left here now."

"There's still the land."

"Oh God, the land. Always the land." Her face glazed over and for a moment, I thought she was going to laugh. "Why is that so important? Why are piles of dead earth worth giving up everything? What about life? What about people?" She hefted a suitcase out of the Jeep and started to walk toward the house.

I wanted to keep quiet, but the words burst forth: "What have you given up? You haven't lived here for years."

She spun back to face me. "I've given up everything and everyone I've ever loved." She blushed deeply, and then her face paled. "Almost everyone."

She picked up her suitcase and hurried into the house. Even in her haste, she stepped around me, moving as if an inner voice prompted her: *keep your distance, don't touch.* When I opened the door, I heard her footsteps ascending the staircase, light and steady as the pattering of raindrops.

I clutched the door handle, frozen by her words. Jenny couldn't forgive me for being here when our brother wasn't. I thought I had gotten over my envy of the closeness they had shared years ago.

I had tried to protect myself from Jenny, hardening my eyes and my heart against her childlike face, her startling green eyes. It wasn't possible, any more than I could avoid the pain I had felt in the last days of Mother's life. I couldn't deny our connection. Hiding from either of them was like hiding from myself.

Jenny often accused me of overlooking her. But I couldn't ignore a being as full of life, as demanding, as Jenny. If I turned away it was because her need cried out to me so sharply. I feared for my sister.

If I traced the generations of women in our family, individual faces stood out less than the legacy of being female, the threads of hope and desire and disappointment that connected us more than our genes. Almost transparent, those bindings were as uncompromising and tough as steel. All through my childhood, at church suppers and neighborhood gatherings, I watched farm women listening patiently to children and men, their faces reflecting concern—for others. I imagined their inner selves, as fragile as bone china, cracking and collapsing a day at a time from neglect. As a young woman, I felt surrounded by a great sea of concealed feeling, of opportunities lost, chances not taken because of unspoken obligations to care for other people. Fear of going under drove me away from rural life.

Jenny spoke of love. How could she know the joy I felt when she was born? Holding the perfect body and head of my baby sister gave me hope I would never be alone again.

As a child, I knew loneliness well. The country seemed even flatter than it is now, the trees shorter, the wind stronger. Like a stalk of wheat, whipped and tossed at the whim of an uncanny god of storms, I stared up into the heart of an August sun. I imagined standing there until I went blind, my skin seared until only my bones, bleached and pure, jutted up from the earth. But when my sister was born, my own flesh took root and came alive.

I ran after Jenny, racing up the steep staircase and into her old room. Startled, she stared at me, her arms filled with clothes from her suitcase. The soft fabrics enfolded her thin wrists, their colors splashing against her pale skin—melon, forest green, muted apricot, sienna brown.

I longed to tell her how much I had wished for her counsel when I didn't know how to take care of Mother. If only I knew how to say, *Jenny, I've needed you.* But I had no words. Dumbly, I watched a turquoise scarf drift out of my sister's arms and float toward the floor. It lay crumpled on the faded gray carpet, a dazzling patch of color in the shape of a star.

Wanting to share with her what I had gone through, I cried out: "I loved that woman whose body you're going to see for the last time. I took care of her and watched her grow old. Do you remember how robust Mother was, how strong? My God, her back was as broad as a man's."

Jenny's large eyes looked soft and naked, as I had seen them so many times. She blinked back tears. I wanted to go to her then and hold her. Instead, I said: "It's easy to care about people who are young and beautiful and full of hope."

She stepped toward me, her thin body so strained I sensed its vibration. "Do you mean David?"

I felt my face grow hot. "I didn't mean anyone."

"You were here when Mother died, and you were the last of us to see David. Just say it. I was never here when they needed me."

I waited, her tension and rage rolling toward me in waves. "You don't need me to say that to you. You say it to yourself, don't you, all the time?"

Jenny bolted by me, down the stairs, and out the front door. From her bedroom window, I saw her cross the road. By the time she reached the wheat field, she was running, her dark-blond hair streaming in the wind. Watching her, I envied her lightness, her speed. Age had not dulled her desire to race, to throw herself upon the air and to slice cleanly through it. Do we want to stay young because we dislike change, or because we just want another chance to try it all again, and make it right this time?

I turned away from the window and turned my back on Jenny's bright clothing, discarded on the bed and the floor. My hand skimmed the smooth maple railing as I made my way back down the stairs. A sad emptiness filled the house.

I had talked with Mother about Jenny not wanting to come back to the place where she grew up. "Your dad was like that," she said. "Always wanted to be anywhere but here. But Jenny can't leave herself behind any more than your dad could. Any more than you could. Pieces of her life are still back on this land."

"Sometimes people lay things down and they like how light it makes them feel," I told her, wondering if Jenny would ever let me help her pick up those pieces.

I remembered how small Jenny was when I picked her up for the first time. And how her few pounds added to mine made me feel just right.

The Dead Know

I haunted the cemetery each time I returned to my hometown. The names on the headstones were a roll call of the families I had known as a child—Thorsgren, Anderson, Nyhus, Svendsen.

I had gone back to see my aunt Vi. She had called last week to say: "Roger, there's a man following me." She had seen him delivering her mail, walking the neighbor's terrier, cleaning the windows across the street. She asked if I could come and visit her really soon. She lived in Grand Forks, North Dakota, and I lived in Minneapolis. A five-hour drive, not terrible.

Aunt Vi peered out one of those old-fashioned peepholes on the top of her front door when I knocked. She looked the same as three months before when I had seen her—cheery blue eyes, a cloud of white curls, pink cheeks, layers of sweaters over some kind of loose blue pants. It was September, so Vi fought the chill most of the time.

"Nephew!" She flashed a smile both dazzling and relieved. "Am I ever glad to see you!" She placed one bony hand on my arm and tugged me inside with surprising force. Aunt Vi still pumped iron at eighty-five. "It worked for Jack LaLanne," she always said. "Remember when he towed a boat across a harbor with his teeth when he turned ninety?"

I couldn't remember if that was true about him being ninety. I think he was closer to sixty. But still. "Aunt Vi, you look terrific."

"Huh," she said. "You always say that, Roger." She gave me the once-over with those searchlight eyes. "You look a little peaky to me. I hate to say it, but you do."

"We're heading into winter," I protested. "Besides, our family is just pale, you know that, except for you." A dimple appeared in Aunt Vi's cheek.

We made our way to the living room. It was five in the afternoon, so Aunt Vi brought out the Scotch and two glasses. She splashed a few fingers into each one. "A tot of this will warm you up," she would often say. Today, she just said: "A tot of this will do us good." Then she raised her glass at me—"Salud!"—and took a hefty swallow.

I drank, but just a sip. Aunt Vi could hold her liquor, so the faster she went, the slower I would go. "Tell me about this man," I said.

"He's kind of like you—peaky-lookin'. Pale, dark hair. Not as handsome a'course."

Her lips turned into a bow—Vi must have been one cute number back in the day. All five feet five inches of her. She still had an hourglass figure. How did she do it? I felt like I needed an iron tonic just thinking about it.

"Did he say anything to you?"

Vi leaned back in her wingchair, stuck her legs straight out in front of her. "Just that he knows me."

"What do you mean?"

"He pointed his finger at me, said 'Lady, you can run but you can't hide from me. I knew your granddaddy, I knew your momma, and I know you.'"

"God, Aunt Vi, this sounds like a Western movie from the 1950s! You're kidding, right?"

"Hell no, Nephew. I am telling you true."

"Well, do you know him?"

Aunt Vi sat up straight, tugged at her pants around her knees. Her white hair looked like it could bounce. "Hell yes, I know him."

"Well, if you know him, maybe he's not following you!" I picked up my Scotch and tipped it back.

Aunt Vi crossed her legs and jiggled the top one. "Roger, you remember the Svendsen family that lived on the farm near your parents?"

"Yes." When your nearest neighbors are a mile away, you know everyone in a five-mile radius as Aunt Vi well knew.

"Well, I dated Magnus Svendsen in high school."

She didn't say anything further. Magnus? I didn't think I knew him. My best pal in the ninth grade was Darryl Svendsen and his dad's name was something like Alvin. So that made Magnus what?

"Spell it out for me, Aunt Vi," I poured another inch of Scotch. "I can't place him."

"Darryl's dad's brother was Magnus. He died two years after high school in a crash at a railroad crossing."

Funny Darryl had never told me about this uncle. I needed to pay attention. Had I missed something? "So . . . Aunt Vi, this man who you know is following you isn't Magnus Svendsen because he's already dead? That's all I can make out."

A rare patient expression crossed Vi's face. "No, it isn't Magnus. But it looks a lot like him."

A twin? I wondered. Magnus had a twin brother?

Thankfully, Aunt Vi didn't make me wait. "Magnus had a best friend. He had a crush on me too. When Magnus died, Arnie moved away. He left here and we never saw him again."

"So now he's come back and he's paying unusual attention to your whereabouts?"

"That's what it seems like to me."

"Uh-huh. But why is this a problem?"

Aunt Vi twisted the top button on the gray heather cardigan she was wearing. "It scares me how much Arnie looks like Magnus sixty-some years later, that's why. It could *be* him. Arnie never forgave any of us that Magnus died and we lived."

I scooched my chair closer to hers and picked up one of her strong hands, the veins ropy and soft. I could see she was upset. I tried to sound soothing: "You don't really know what Magnus would look like now. It was probably very sad when he died. But it was a long time ago."

A tear splashed down Vi's cheek. Her voice was still strong. "Young man, just because something was a long time ago doesn't mean it can't hurt as much as it ever did."

I nodded. I was forty-eight. I wasn't young, but it was nice that my aunt still thought so.

"I was in that car the night Magnus crashed. Two of my girlfriends were with us. He sat in the backseat—we were racing across those tracks, a little drunk, a lot silly. We thought beating the train was hilarious." She shut her eyes and slumped. "We almost outran that train, but it glanced the rear of our car and that's where Magnus was sitting."

I could see hulking metal bearing down on my aunt as she strained forward in the seat.

"You were riding in front?" The mysteries of fate punched me in the chest. "Thank God you made it."

Aunt Vi's face collapsed around her mouth and jaw. She shook her head, opened her mouth, but released only air. "I . . . I wish I hadn't," she finally managed.

"But, gosh. It was an accident. I mean . . ."

Her blue eyes searched my face and then looked away at the living room wall. A Delft plate with the silhouette of two children curving toward each other graced the striped wallpaper.

The air thinned between us, and I felt my aunt's extra years melt toward me. "Oh, Aunt Vi . . ." My stomach tumbled. I saw those sturdy hands gripping the wheel as if they were my own.

The Last Usher

After Edgar Allan Poe

Before I was born, my mother built a labyrinth in the heart of our property. It became her spiritual center, or perhaps her sacred repository. For I came to believe that a sister, born before my twin brother and I entered this world, lay buried there. Like most family secrets, this one did not rest in peace.

My mother was the writer Madeline Marie Usher. You may remember her books about a pair of twins living on a rambling estate near Lake Superior. Her imagined setting shared none of the gloom of our actual family home, but her stories did mirror the twists and turns of the labyrinth that began at the end of the garden and extended into the grove beyond. I was her namesake, as my brother Roderick was our father's.

Mother read to me often from her work, sitting on the rose divan in her sitting room, her ash-blond hair gathered in a French twist. Her tuneful voice slid easily into dialects and voices.

One story began like this: "The little girl, lost in the great wood, kept going on the twisting path in the hope of finding her brother . . ."

"Wait!" I anxiously looked at her. "Were they twins like Roderick and me?"

"Oh, yes, of course. That's why she couldn't leave the woods. Not without him."

"What might happen if she'd left him?"

"Oh, we can't even think of it." Mother pursed her lips and looked grave. The silk sleeves of her dressing gown rustled like the crush of dry leaves. "Because these twins had to be together. If something happened to one, well, then something happened to the other."

"Was the brother wounded? Or did he die? And then what happened to the little girl?"

Her voice dropped at this. "Madeline, you're rushing the story!" Seeing my face crumple, she added: "Don't worry, she found him in the shallows of a broad stream. She pulled him out and they both lived without incident until . . . Well, that will keep for another day."

"Oh, but you have to tell me now!" I cried.

"Hush, now. And learn to listen. A storyteller can't be forced to speak. A story is like an instrument—it must be coaxed to play its tune." As Mother reached out to touch my face, the silver charms on her bracelet chimed like tiny bells.

Next to the bookcase by her bed was a small photograph showing Mother holding a child with a heart-shaped face and fair hair. Mother looked young in the picture, perhaps only eighteen.

The first time I noticed it, I asked: "Is that Aunt May?" My mother's younger sister had died many years ago; this child had Mother's wide-spaced eyes and high forehead.

Mother plucked at a long strand of creamy pearls at her throat. She stared at the photograph and then turned it facedown on the table. She shook her head.

I reached for the frame, but she stayed my four-year-old fingers with a firm touch. "No, not May. A friend's little girl."

I wasn't satisfied by this answer, but Mother was finished talking about it. She took me by the hand, and we passed through her sitting room and into the hallway. The next time I peered into her bedroom to watch her pinning her hair back, the portrait was gone.

$\sim$

I had fled the weight of Usher House's secrets in my early twenties. But twenty years later, a panicked phone call from my cousin Anne in Minnesota drew me back. "It's Roderick. He's barricaded himself in the house and won't come out."

I picked at the keys of my Steinway, immersed in a thorny phrase in a new composition. "He likes his own company best, you know that."

"He's going the way of our grandfather. And your father. He can't sleep, he seems in a dream even when awake, and—"

"Can he still hear?" My father had lost both sight and hearing by the end of his illness.

"Even the ticking of a clock drives him into fury."

I scoured the skin under my eyes with my fingertips.

"You must come, Madeline. He needs help and you're the only one who can persuade him to get it."

Anne shared my brother's fascination with the old house—and his certainty of its coming destruction. The place had always seemed more a container of morbid fantasies than a shelter. Its twin turrets loomed over the landscape like coffins. My grandfather's rants about floods and contagions had graced many a childhood meal. I couldn't help but wonder that a family so emotionally tone-deaf to one another could be so attuned to the heavy footfalls of disaster approaching.

Anne's clogged breathing irritated my ear, and I shifted the phone to the other side of my head. Her asthma flared up every autumn, and the pressure to speak caused her to wheeze. The creative wave I had been riding for the past few hours had crashed with her news. I didn't want to go back to Usher, but an old urge drove me on. My cousin's appeal was like offering a drug to an addict—once the suggestion had taken root that my brother needed rescue and that only I could manage it, it was already too late.

Regret crept over me as I saw the life I had carefully carved out for myself receding.

Yet I tried to resist: "He'll come out when he's ready. I really don't see what good my coming—"

"It's not only Roderick," Anne interrupted.

"What then?"

"There's someone trapped in there with him."

Someone could only be Jonathan, my brother's special friend.

Until he brought Jonathan home with him from college the Christmas of 1972, the year we turned twenty-one, my brother never invited anyone to our house. I came home as well that holiday, nerves afire at the thought of the coming visitor.

When Jonathan appeared at the door, I saw the violin case in his hand. Any shyness I had vanished. "We can all play together," I said.

"Violin?" he asked.

"Piano," I replied.

That he and Roderick made music together showed their rare connection. My brother had inherited hearing so acute that noise of any kind, even most music, was intolerable to him. When we were growing up, Roderick had three fans in his bedroom to mask sound, complaining he could hear mice scratching in the attic two floors above. There was one exception: Roderick's nerves calmed to the sound of stringed instruments. The cello was his first love. The violin, second. The piano, in spite of its percussive qualities, his third.

My twin and I spent many long Minnesota winters playing together in our father's library. With Jonathan's arrival that December, we were three.

Jonathan's gifts were many. Dark-haired and small, Jonathan wore brocade vests in deep vermillion that accentuated his slim waist. His skin gleamed like polished stone. Even in the dimness of the library he shone, an exotic creature. The sound his fingers coaxed from his strings dispelled the cold and damp. The house itself favored Jonathan—the honey-colored wainscoting in the room matched his skin, the Corot on the wall behind him surrounded his brightness with mist and cloud. Neither Roderick nor I had ever played half so well.

My brother too was handsome. You might think that I, as his twin, shared this physical grace. But I felt diminished by the striking males in the room that winter, conscious that my hands were too large, my nose not distinguished. Thank God for Schumann and Schubert to concentrate on. For I loved Jonathan, even though Roderick had already claimed him.

That winter marked the kind of crossroads for our family that your mind records only years later when you turn to see the path forking behind you. Those days live on for me encased in an aura of perfection. Yes, there was the beautiful Jonathan to torment me, but my father and mother were alive, and Usher House was still majestic in its way, its three stories jutting toward the sky as if to make a point.

I still shiver when I recall the erotic current firing among us during those hours in the library, the notes leaping from our fingers and changing the tenor of the air itself. The afternoon light glazed Jonathan's hair as he bent over his violin, his head tilted toward Roderick. "So fine," I can still hear him murmur. Was he speaking about the music or feeling the caress of my brother's eyes?

In the years since, I've pictured Jonathan as a prodigy with the charisma of a Liszt or a Chopin transported into the mercantile mania of the late twentieth century. Not a year has gone by since that I haven't wished to see him again, even though what I had hoped for never took place, not the musical triumphs, nor the return of my affection.

Roderick and I may have been twins, but Jonathan's eyes sought only my brother. Perhaps that was for the best, because disappointment released me from Usher. Grief is a great teacher. Life had led me to other places and other homes in the two decades since—North Carolina, Wales, the Florida Keys, and now California—but never back to live in Usher House.

Urged on by my cousin's alarm, I drove through a fine mist. The September colors along the St. Croix were radiant in the afternoon light. It was the kind of weather Roderick liked best. In our twinship, he was the moon and I the sun—he craved the dark as much as I welcomed the light.

I reached the end of what used to be a smooth drive of paving stones. A tangle of brush and weeds now flanked the road once adorned by oaks and alder. Fifty years ago, Usher House had been grand, twenty years ago merely stately, until now "shabby" and "quaint" were a distant memory. If Father had been with me, the sight of Usher's decline would have robbed him of any sense he had left. If houses are dreams of the life we hope for, then Usher had been his greatest dream. It takes so long to build something fine, and the mere flick of a finger for it to collapse around you.

My rented Volvo felt stable and safe, so much so that when I parked in the gravel drive outside the front door, I was reluctant to leave it. Outside, the red and yellow leaves burnished the walk in the late autumn light. The brickwork was stained and cracked. Some dead ivy clung to the north side of the house. "Ivy-covered" is a description that implies coziness, but the ivy that had once thickly carpeted the exterior had died back, leaving yellow-stained filaments and black twigs. It resembled a scourge slowly squeezing the life out of the house. Rot can begin either outside or in, but the end result is the same.

The autumn light retreated from the sky. I had left California only that morning yet already my trip stretched to a weary length. Leaving the comfort of the Volvo, I made my way up the walk. At the door, I tipped my head back. The third floor blocked the very sun.

I knocked to no effect, waited, then pressed the bell. A melodious chiming echoed throughout the house. Seconds later, a scream erupted from the hallway.

A ravaged face appeared at the door. "That terrible sound—the workers promised me they'd sever the wire!" Swept back from a high forehead, my brother's hair gave him the air of a maestro in full conducting mode.

His watery blue eyes took me in. "Madeline? Oh my God, Madeline!" His jaw tightened and for a moment I feared an angry outburst. Then he fell upon my neck, sobbing.

I held my brother, hoping he couldn't hear how my heart threatened to shatter the cage of my ribs. His frailty frightened me. Surely time could not be so cruel? Excusing myself for a moment, I splashed water on my face and neck and held a cloth against my eyes in the dark bathroom by the kitchen. I willed myself into steadiness.

Roderick was waiting for me when I came out, his smile eager. I followed him into the library. Books still filled the shelves, their leather bindings retaining a gloss even while damp stained the ceiling. My piano was confined to a dim corner, covered with a cloth. Without asking if I wanted any, he poured us each a glass of sherry.

I had to keep reminding myself that this creature, only forty-one years old, was my brother: the thin wrists poking out of his white shirt, the shaking hands, the wasted face. He sat crookedly in my father's favorite settee, the upholstery retaining only a tinge of its once-vivid green.

Roderick's skin was ghostly in the candlelight, for one of my brother's phobias was electric light. Pocked with shadows from the uneven glow of a dozen candles, the library seemed a tinderbox with its long draperies and acres of dry pages. If I expressed to Roderick my worries about the room catching fire, he would only dismiss my fears with more irritation.

"You look well." His hungry eyes searched my face.

"Thank you. You—" I couldn't possibly return the compliment. "You've been ill."

"Ah, ill." His fingers, as delicate and expressive as ever, passed over his eyes. "You can't imagine what it's been like. Living here, everything falling around my ears."

I shivered and resisted the urge to rush toward him, gather up his slender frame, and run into the night. "Tell me. What can I do to help you?"

Roderick sighed and shook his head. "What could anyone ever do?" He looked vacant for a moment, his blue eyes washed-out. Tears leaked onto his cheeks. He slammed his glass down with a desperate strength. The crystal shattered. "There's no point to any of it."

I hurried over to him, perched at the edge of the divan, and stroked his hair, once the texture and color of corn silk. The now-coarse strands were the only sturdy thing about him.

Touching Roderick's hair brought back the Christmas Jonathan had spent with us twenty years before, Jonathan's glossy dark head erect above his violin, my brother's fingers plying the cello strings as his fine features angled toward his friend. I sat at the piano, slightly outside the current that united them. My brother's hair then flowed from the crown of his head like the music: fine and true, a thing of beauty.

~

Roderick and I were the only offspring of our parents, the last of our branch of Ushers. Father had been an only child. Mother's sister had died of a virus that decimated the Canadian village where they had grown up. My cousin Anne was the daughter of Mother's stepsister. Anne, whose surname was Newland, gave me hope in many ways; she had two daughters of her own, just one year apart.

Roderick had left Usher for college only at the urging of our father. He came home immediately after taking his degree and moved back in with our parents, having developed a passion for all things medieval. In a fever of energy, he expanded the library, a great room on the main floor that had been my grandfather's pride. He then spent all of his attention tracking down obscure texts. Once a month he entertained other scholars who came to pore with him over a rare codex rescued from an attic or crypt. I often imagined my brother in a carrel at the dawn of the Renaissance, keening phrases as he copied them onto parchment. My brother, you see, seemed far from the mid-twentieth century when he had been born, and impossibly distant from the twenty-first.

Father had succumbed to a stroke at sixty in the late 1980s. His death may have been sudden, but his illness was long. The disease that tortured generations of men in our family began with tremors and swings of mood, then progressed to complete disability. Drugs and lethargy ate him from the inside before the disease rendered him inert.

Mother died two years later, at only fifty-five, whether from grief or despair I cannot say. Always prone to migraines, my mother spent the last year of her life locked away in the west wing of the main floor in the one truly charming room on the estate. Marked by high ceilings and broad casement windows, the room faced a garden that she had once cultivated like an acolyte tending a sacred site.

Laced with crushed shell paths, graced by willows and gauzy maples, the garden offered a rare profusion of hope. I often wondered if growing the brilliant red and yellow tulips, the wine-colored poppies, the borders of thyme and tarragon had been her only pleasure. That, and her beloved books.

After Father died, worry about Mother brought me back to Usher every three months. Once she had immersed herself in reading and writing, but now she planted herself in an armchair and moped at the windows to her garden, despairing as weeds and vines consumed her once-beloved plot of ground. My intrepid mother refused to open the house to birdsong or the rush of wind in the trees. She grew torpid and dull.

"I can't go out there," she would say when I offered to walk with her among the still-surviving plants. "Not now. I blame myself for what happened to your father. The herbs I gave him. I thought they would salve his fever, but no . . . he became more delirious, more fitful."

"But all the doctors said there was no treatment. They couldn't find a cause and therefore could discover no cure."

At this, she looked at me above her half-moon glasses, her gray eyes murky against the bright light outside. "Do you really believe that, Madeline?"

"I do."

She sighed, smoothing the brown silk of her dress over her knees. "Well, it happened to his father before him and his before that. It's a family wasting, beyond the grasp of the medical mind."

At first, I attributed her decline to the toll caring for Father had taken during his long illness. The family malady that claimed the males of each generation—deteriorating nerves, overly acute hearing followed by deafness, weight loss, and finally seizures—had never been diagnosed. Doctors were summoned, then, puzzled, they eventually gave up.

Once engrossed in her gardens and writing, the study of herbs and their application, always reading the latest in history and poetry, Mother grew listless and dull. She hadn't been able to help her husband with medicinal plants: feverfew, valerian, bloodroot, dewdrops harvested from a wide border along the courtyard outside her rooms.

"Madeline," she greeted me a month before she died. She had held her arms before her like a sleepwalker. I had embraced her and taken her outside into the autumn sun.

"You're so pale, Mother. You can't stay inside like this with the drapes drawn. You, always drawn to the sun, to weather, wind, rain. I remember dancing with you during violent storms growing up." I had a vision of her, face toward the sky, raindrops streaming through her hair, the moisture seeming to dissolve the years and restore youth to her skin.

First, she confined herself to only one walk in the morning, instead of the hours and hours consulting with the gardener, tending one flower bed and another. She would disappear into the labyrinth she had built on the outskirts of the property, insisting no one follow her inside its convoluted pathways. Gradually she stopped walking altogether.

"Mother, the labyrinth, you promised to tell me what was buried in the center, I—"

"We won't speak of that," she spoke sharply. "No one is ever to go into the labyrinth again. I'm thinking of having George seal it off."

My brother Roderick, isolated in his own regimen in his library, rarely appeared. "We must help her," I told him on a rare evening when I found him in the parlor drinking wine.

"Help?" He cocked his head to one side as if needing time to consider. He shook his head. "You know it's no use. She's made up her mind. You must let her be." He gave me a fierce look. "Allow her privacy at least."

His gnomic pronouncements drove me to exasperation. "A mere half year ago this was a vital woman! What do you mean she's made up her mind? To do what?"

"You know very well, Madeline. She hears voices you can't discern. And sees things that guide her. She has chosen her path." When I stared at him, astonished, he threw up his hands and scolded: "You have no imagination!"

His clothing looked disheveled; he too seemed to be losing weight. "Oh, for heaven's sake, she needs medical help! Tell me at least who she has consulted."

He smiled then and pointed to a notebook on the table next to him. But when I reached for it, he snatched it out of my reach and tucked it into the inner pocket of his vest. "This is private. Trust me when I say she's seen the best medical minds of this entire region."

He was so smug, so full of secrets, so completely irritating. Did he not care about his own mother? I left him sipping his red wine, staring at the ceiling, playing a piece of music in his head, or dreaming about another century. Who could decipher the logic of his thinking?

I left him and knocked at the sitting room door to my mother's quarters. She had three rooms, all on the west side of the house. She spent her days in the sitting room and kept her dried plant cuttings and records in the small room that served as a passageway to her bedroom. That grand room had a corner fireplace, a huge four-poster bed, and a nightstand always piled high with books.

It was ten-thirty. Perhaps she had retired. But as I waited in the hallway, surrounded by the gloomy oils of the Usher ancestors winking in the weak light, I heard footsteps, then the rustling of her silk robe, and she opened the door.

She took off her half glasses and peered at me. "Madeline." She sounded surprised to see me even though we had shared dinner three hours before.

She had dressed with care for dinner this evening and looked better and more animated than I had seen her for some weeks. But now I was struck by the severity of her face, pulled down by worry or fatigue or perhaps the fear that her life was leaking away. For she looked much aged in these three hours. I resisted the urge to check my watch to see the date. Surely this wasn't the same person I had dined with scant hours ago.

"Do you ever sleep, Mother?" I blurted. "You seem very tired."

She sighed, a sound of leaves rattling together in a slight wind. Her shoulders bent forward, which I had never noticed before. "Sleep is not so easy for me now. If it is for you, enjoy it while you can." She looked closely at me. "You've certainly grown up, Madeline. I've always thought of you as so young."

I was only thirty-six and her comment startled me. "I'm old enough to worry about you," I said. "Something is very wrong. I'm hoping you'll talk to me about it. I'm leaving in two days and I'm so very worried . . ."

She took my face in her hands as she used to when I was a child. "You have so much ahead of you. Do not worry about your old mother."

"Old? But you're not, not at all. Are you ill?"

She stood away from the door so that I could enter. I followed her as she sat on the maroon chaise and sat opposite her on a squat upholstered chair. "I don't know how to tell you," she began.

I waited, for when I had been impatient as a child, she had told me that pressuring her grated on her senses like careless hands pounding on a piano. I didn't want her to turn away from me now.

"When your father was so ill, I'm afraid I didn't get enough rest and I began to have violent headaches. Then vertigo. I went to my doctor, of course, and he couldn't find a cause. But he sent me for tests. They discovered a brain tumor."

She appeared resigned but I grasped both of her hands. "What about surgery? Or radiation?"

Turning her head away, she stared at a portrait of Father on the wall. "The doctors monitored the tumor. I'm afraid it began to grow. It's too embedded to be removed safely."

"But there must be other treatments. You can't just give up." Inside, a voice clamored *don't leave*.

"I am resigned. My headaches worsen." She remained silent for some time. "I didn't save your father, Madeline."

At a loss, I tried to coax her out of her quarters. "Come, let's go out in the fresh air at least. You can't just sit here regretting something you never had the power to change."

"*Change*, Madeline. A word that is easy to say, but for me, impossible to achieve." At that, she rose and drew the curtains on the garden window. I noticed how stiff her carriage was, how halting her gait. That was the last time I ever saw my mother.

~

I hadn't returned to Usher these three years since her death. Without her, the hush of the house seemed profound. And unnatural.

In the library, Roderick grasped my hand and leaned toward me. "Ghosts, Madeline, they crowd around me."

An antique violin stood in a far corner of the room on a platform, dusty and forlorn. When we were young, we heard my grandfather playing it at night when he couldn't sleep. An unused instrument is a sad ghost all by itself.

"Tell me." I wanted to ask about Jonathan.

I had trouble hearing Roderick then, but I think he said: "A ghost is nothing but a truth you're afraid to see."

"What?

The air shifted in the room. My head swung toward the doorway. An emaciated form stepped forward. Was it one of the wraiths my father claimed haunted the library?

"Madeline." The baritone voice was still clear. "I knew you'd come."

I was afraid to close my eyes, afraid that if I blinked, he would be gone, for it was Jonathan framed in the doorway.

I couldn't help myself. I rushed toward him, arms wide. But he took a step back. "Best not to get too close," he said and coughed. The cough at first seemed discreet, like punctuation, but then grew into a horrible hack. His arms flailed out as if dispersing a cloud of bees. "Excuse me," he croaked as he turned away. I heard his feet on the stairs, not rushing but steady.

I whirled around. "What's happened?" My brother sat, his hand over his heart. Roderick had our father's disease, but surely Jonathan, no relative at all . . .

"He's dying."

"He looks all of about a hundred pounds. What's wrong with him?"

Roderick shook his head. "He's seen so many doctors. Specialists, too."

Specialists. My father had consulted a long line of them to no effect. I saw again my mother closing the drapes to the garden, mentioning the herbs she had given him because there was no help to be had.

But Jonathan—did he have cancer? Tuberculosis? AIDS?

My brother's eyes glistened with fever. Sweat stood out on his forehead. "I wish . . ." He began to hum softly.

"Roderick, talk to me." But he looked at me vacantly and smiled. The humming continued.

The tuneless sound—from such a master musician as my brother—shocked me. My grandfather and my father did this too as their illness progressed, lapsing from clarity into delirium in the time it took to stumble off a curb.

Retaking my seat next to Roderick, I again took his hand, trying for calm. "You didn't give him anything, did you, from Mother's garden?"

"The garden," his voice wistful. "It was beautiful when we were young. And then Mother let it go . . . didn't she?"

"Yes, she did. But remember certain plants still grew along the wall. We tried to get rid of them, but they came back every year."

He nodded. "The lacey ones with the pale tops? Yes, I always liked those. They seemed to help Jonathan. At first."

My grip tightened around his creased skin. "I don't think they're safe. We must have them tested right away."

He ripped his hand away from mine. "No! You're not allowed to pick them. And no one must come here. What do you mean 'have them tested'?" He laughed. "Silly Madeline. Dreamy Madeline. You don't understand."

The insult stung. I was silly, when I was the one who had escaped Usher, a feat that had required planning and skill? I pushed that thought aside. "Perhaps I don't. Explain it to me."

"It's the house." His eyes turned shrewd. "It wants Jonathan. Just like it wants me." He peered over his shoulder. "The house always gets what it wants. And it wants to be fed."

"Surely it didn't want Mother." The lack of her was in the dusty frames of the portraits, the eerie quiet in the halls, the absence of a pulse everywhere. She had been gone only three years, but love had ebbed away from Usher with her passing. In the shadows I still saw her rapt face gazing at the garden, her deep focus as she pored over her notebooks.

Roderick's head lolled back against the settee. "She wasn't exempt, you know. No one is. Don't forget that she built the labyrinth and buried a part of herself there. She gave the house permission."

My old fear about the fate of the little girl in Mother's photograph sharpened my tone. "What was buried there? Or should I say who?"

"You know we don't talk about anything we can't see in this house. But, feel free, look for yourself."

My brother's riddles began to give me a headache. "I need to rest for a bit."

"I wouldn't sleep in Mother's room if I were you." Roderick's head dipped forward.

I slid from the divan and left the library. My feet traveled the familiar path down the hall to Mother's room. The dark portraits of my father's family winked in the dim lighting. *Don't laugh at me*, I thought. *I'm not trapped on these walls.*

I stopped and listened for Jonathan moving above me in my brother's quarters.

But all was silent.

The heavy door at the end of the hall had been the gateway to the magic of my mother's company. When I was a child, no day was too dull to resist the sparkle of her words, the keenness of her glance. A residue of warmth still radiated outward from the wood to my hand.

I turned the tarnished brass knob, but the door did not open. I braced my shoulder against it, but still the door didn't give way. For a moment I thought I would have to rouse Roderick for the key. But then I remembered that the door locked only from the inside. I knew that Jonathan was upstairs, and my brother dozed in the library. No one else was in the house. I feared that my mother's spirit had sealed her chambers.

Registering that thought appeared to give me sanction to enter, because immediately the door swung wide. "Hello?" I called into the silence.

Mother's sitting room was as I remembered it, the wallpaper a cream-and-rose swirl, the furnishings a simple velvet loveseat and chaise. A glass-topped table still held books and a pair of half glasses. Heavy burgundy draperies covered the floor to ceiling windows that looked over the garden.

A dressing room separated the sitting room from the bedroom. As I walked through this passageway, I smelled lemon and thyme, a hint of honeysuckle. Shelves holding bins of crushed herbs, pulverized roots, and dried leaves lined those walls. My mother had long studied the properties of plants and mixed concoctions to keep us all healthy. Her petri dishes and crucible were still at the far end of her bedroom. These and the Bunsen burner she called her "chemistry." She would cook her concoctions over an open flame, staining the ceilings with soot and smudging the drapes.

Mother had never acclimated to the damp winters. I saw her still in her four-poster bed, her small frame encased in heavy woolen quilts. The bedroom held a varnished black table; on it a row of notebooks stood between marble horsehead bookends. Mother kept records of all plantings in the garden, the ordering of bulbs and seeds, notes about rootstock. I selected one slim black book and opened it at random: May 6, 1975. On that day alone, the gardener had planted over a hundred bulbs, weeded a quarter acre of turf.

"Common plants are underestimated," Mother often said, her face serene. "The berries of lantana, foxglove leaves, the young larkspur, even daffodil bulbs—those and many more can be fatal. Don't interfere with my plants, Madeline. Do you promise?"

Horrified to know that the garden I played in could be toxic, I could only nod. "What if the leaves poison you when you touch them?"

She smiled then. "I'm very careful, little one. Don't worry about me."

The entries on the page entranced me. Fully fifty common houseplants grown at Usher could be fatal in sufficient quantities. It would be child's play for Roderick to crush a few seeds, shave a sliver from a bulb or a berry, and drop them into Jonathan's food. But why would Roderick sicken the person he loved most in the world?

Because he is ill. Because he doesn't want to die alone. The surety of truth pierced my brain: Roderick was poisoning Jonathan and himself *because that death was far better than the ones they were headed toward.*

If only Mother were alive to tell me what I should do. I hurried back into her sitting room and opened the curtains. When I switched on the outdoor lights, only a few lamps shone in the strings of lights that once had illuminated the garden paths. The wind had come up; rampant vines and weeds twisted together high in the air. The elm tree branches curved to meet them. The limbs and stalks appeared to be dancing, a wild arrhythmic ballet in the night.

And then I fancied I saw a shape moving away from the house, a blur of white. No, not a ghost, but a frail human being. The figure could only be Jonathan.

Cold air and spitting rain greeted me as I opened the casement windows and stepped into the garden. Plants whipped across my face—warning slaps urging me back. Usher House might be unstable, but all order ended at its walls. Outside another sensibility ruled. I thought of King Lear on the heath raging against fate in a storm. Rage, at our impotence against nature's force, seemed an apt response as barbed branches cut through my clothing and I stumbled on the slick stones along the path.

I reached the far end of what had once been cultivated. Beyond was Mother's labyrinth, which led into the woods. I saw the occasional shimmer of white ahead of me.

"Jonathan!" I screamed into the wind and rain. "Come back!" He was in no condition to survive the storm, or to find his way.

Seeing where he was headed, I remembered asking Mother over and over the summer I was ten: "What are you making?" From the garden to the grove, a distance of perhaps a quarter mile, a crew planted hedges in a pattern, expanding the maze that was there into something much more elaborate.

"I once walked the Chartres labyrinth. In France. I've never felt so calm since. But this one is special." Her lips stretched into a secret smile, one I had caught her sometimes sharing with my father.

"Can I see what is so special?"

"No, you must not go there." Her eyebrows drew together as if she were in pain. "Something is buried at the center, you see, something no one must touch but me."

That made no sense. Why bury something there when there were acres of garden to dig in? It made no sense, but it frightened me. "Is it our cat?" Our tabby had died the year before.

"Madeline, what have I said? I'm not ready to tell you, but I promise I will someday."

I thought of the portrait of the girl with my very young mother that had disappeared when I was four and had haunted me ever since. I didn't dare voice my greatest fear—what if Mother had birthed another little girl before me? And what if that girl had died? I imagined a bit of myself lay there with her. In stories of the old families cherished children died and were sealed in a crypt on the property. Was I alive because she was not? I believed that the middle of the labyrinth was the core of Usher, radiating heat just like Mother's heart.

"I can see you're thinking morbid thoughts." Mother's hand rested firmly on my shoulder. "You must trust me to have my own secrets. This one has nothing to do with you." Her tone had a final edge. "Do you hear me?"

I nodded, but of course I had gone into the labyrinth after Mother declared it finished. I had followed our dog inside and gotten lost, because unlike the Chartres construction, which guides the worshipper in gentle circles to its core, this one had many false endings and traps. Mother found me weeping in a tributary that ended in a sinkhole. Just out of my reach my dog was losing a fight in the quicksand. Together we got him out just in time.

But now in the storm, I caught up to the stumbling figure in the first circle of the labyrinth. It was Jonathan in white pajamas. Like a sleep-walker, his brow was untroubled, and he had a smile on his face.

Gently, I hooked my arm in his and turned him around. "It's too cold out here."

"Madeline." He touched my cheek and then drew his hand away, a look of wonder on his face. "I knew you'd come."

He had said that to me in the library. Did he not remember he had already seen me? I attempted to soothe him: "Of course I'm here."

"It was so hot, I had to come outside." He twisted around. "What is this place?" Oblivious to the treacherous ground that could swallow him whole, he seemed attracted to it just the same.

I guided him firmly away. "Just some paths Mother built. Nothing, really. Come, let's get back."

"I'm so very thirsty," he said. "I thought some fresh air, this lovely rain . . ."

Jonathan's hair was plastered to his head, the strands twisting like the plants surrounding us. He allowed me to steer him back in the direction of the garden, but his body trembled in agitation. "Did you ever write me? All those years ago?"

Hadn't he received the dozens of letters I had written? "Oh, yes. Don't you remember, we were going to meet when you were touring in Chicago that first winter after you'd been here?"

He frowned. "But why didn't we?"

The ache inside me sharpened, still bitter after all these years. I had waited for him at a restaurant on Michigan Avenue that night for hours. It had been raining and cold, just like this night. "I don't know," I whispered.

"But, listen. I did want to see you." He massaged his forehead. "Oh, if I only could tell you . . ."

"What? I would've given anything to see you."

He stopped and touched me, both of his hands framing my face this time. "Roderick was with me. He didn't feel well. I wish I could make you understand, but . . ."

"Yes?"

"Whenever Roderick isn't well, neither am I. It's the same for both of us. I wish it weren't so. But the two of us, I'm not sure that we are two, I . . ."

His voice trailed off; a melancholy smile twisted his still-lovely mouth. I thought of him playing a Bach sonata, the notes fading into the quiet and melting our hearts.

"I'm so sorry, Madeline." Without warning, his gaunt body began sprinting toward Usher House. He held up an arm, the hand seeming to say: *don't follow.*

But of course, I followed, just as I had gone into Mother's labyrinth, just as I had handled the plants she told me never to touch, and just as when we were all twenty-one, I ran up to Roderick's room one morning excited about the day only to find him and Jonathan lying in each other's arms.

I ran after Jonathan because if I stood still, I might feel my own heart breaking.

I don't know how Jonathan stayed ahead of me—I was at least four inches taller than he was, and much stronger. It reminded me of the sudden fits of vitality that seized my father during his illness, his emaciated body rearing up and striking back at the world one more time.

But then Jonathan vanished. My vision blurred in the rain. Roderick's words about the house wanting to be fed echoed in my mind.

When I arrived back at the west wing once again, no one was there. I wondered if Jonathan had fallen along the way. I would have to go back for him. But then a shadow moved along the hallway through the floor to ceiling windows on that side of the house, and I realized he had slipped inside a secret door near my mother's room, a recessed door that most people would have to stoop to enter. Unless they were as small as Jonathan.

Too many things happened then, all at once. There are moments when time warps and you can only follow. White flashed through the window as the figure headed for the stairs. A car engine accelerated; brakes squealed as the vehicle sped around the last curves to Usher. A black sedan swung into the yard in a skid of gravel and my cousin Anne stormed out of the car. She was winded as if she had been running rather than driving.

"Madeline, thank God!" She gripped both of my arms and pulled me toward her.

"I'm glad you're here," I said, "I need help. They're both so sick."

She leaned toward me, still holding one of my arms so tightly that it hurt. "I was so afraid I wouldn't get here in time. I came as soon as I saw the fire . . ."

"What fire? But it's raining." As soon as I spoke, I noticed the rain had stopped. The air felt dry and crisp. It was as if I had taken a detour into another night and returned into this one. I couldn't trust my senses yet what else did I have? Above me the third floor was alight. An angry tide of orange arced into the sky in a freakish pattern, like tongues radiating out to form the top half of a mandala. I couldn't hear the sound of beams falling, yet the very air vibrated as if the fire had a frequency too high to hear.

"The rain stopped hours ago. The trucks should be here any minute. I called them as soon as I saw it . . ." Anne still struggled for breath.

I thrashed against her confining grip. "Come! Help me get them out."

"There's no time."

"What are you saying?" As if stirred by her words, the flames now erupted out of the dormer windows on the second floor and raced down the staircase onto the ground floor. I imagined Roderick waking in the library, gasping for air. And Jonathan, trapped upstairs, embers igniting the carpets, the drapes, his white pajamas . . .

"I'm going in." I strained to break free of her, but Anne hung on with a strange strength. Soon I was too weak to resist my cousin's grip. To think I had once thought Anne's nerves were as brittle as my brother's.

The ravenous fire consumed the walls, until the windows imploded with a roar. We watched in bleak silence.

"Look, this is the end of it," Anne said minutes later. "It must have started hours ago."

"It can't have. I was with Roderick in the library until 9:00 p.m." I looked at my watch. Something was wrong with the thing; its hands pointed to two in the morning. Where had I been for five hours? I had only gone into Mother's wing of the house, looked at the notebooks for a moment, spent scarcely any time at all . . . I turned around slowly, wishing I could reassemble the fractured night.

"It's not possible," I began. "I went into Mother's rooms, for just a few minutes. The bins still held herbs, all labeled as they always were. You remember how it was."

"Yes." Anne's voice was gentle. "I remember that you'd go in there and not come out for hours. Me too. It was mesmerizing. I always thought that room was bewitched. Maybe it was the smell of the plants. Maybe we'd fall asleep. Somehow the day would be gone."

"No. Listen. Jonathan was running toward the labyrinth. I followed him. We talked but not for long. Maybe an hour went by . . ."

I remembered Mother leaning over her Bunsen burner, turning a glass pipe in the flame. "Mother's chemistry! Maybe the fire started there!" But as soon as I spoke, another vision came, of my brother turning in his sleep in the library, an arm thrashing out as he dreamed, knocking over a candle, which fell to the floor in a shower of sparks. My eyes searched the west wing, now a blazing cascade of rubble.

"Step back!" Anne yelled as a gust of wind whipped the flames. Her restraining arm kept me away from Roderick and Jonathan as I strained to go toward them.

In front of us, the house shuddered. As if they were melting, the wings off the hall slid to the ground in a torrent of ash and disintegrating stone.

I slipped on the coarse gravel and crashed to the ground. Above me, Anne's face glistened in the cold air as she held out a hand. I refused to take it. Rocks pricked my knees as I sprawled on the path. I was too weak to ever get up again.

The portraits of the Ushers on the walls glimmered in front of me, and the faces of my grandfather, my father, poor Roderick, dear Jonathan. "They wanted so much to keep it," I said.

"Yes, they wanted Usher too much." For a moment, Anne resembled my mother standing there, strangely calm in the face of great turmoil.

"When you crave something that intensely, you give up your power. You feed it to the thing you desire, until there's nothing left," I said dumbly as ash and bits of wood caught in the wind and twisted like tiny birds, flying up and up in the night air.

"That's not true for you, Madeline."

Silent, I watched the soot swirl and settle.

"Madeline, listen to me, Usher can't take you, not now. You have a future." Tears marked her cheeks, and I wondered if she was thinking of her children.

I looked up at her. The rocks bit into my legs like knives. My skin felt raw and burned. "You can't have a future without the past."

My cousin meant well, but she didn't know what she was saying. The house wasn't just my home—it stood for my family and my history as well. Its walls had enclosed all the people I had loved.

What had Roderick said to me in the library? *A ghost is nothing but a truth you're afraid to see.* I hadn't seen anything, not until now.

Anne didn't understand about Usher House. I had been able to leave it behind only because I had known it was still there. I gripped her shoulders. "Without Usher, how will we know who we are?"

She shook her head—there was no language—and I followed her to her car. A few sparks filtered through the air as we drove away, or was it a sprinkle of stars?

~

I no longer drive the winding road through the Minnesota countryside to visit Usher House. Its ruined walls couldn't be repaired, and the debris was hauled away years ago. But Mother's garden came back, slowly at first and then in rampant palettes of color. The conservatory of the new structure faces it now. The rosy crushed granite paths wander through the plants and the groves, steering one's feet across wildness and possibility.

Anne and her daughters live with me now in the new house, its broad walls and pitched roofs more Craftsman than Victorian in style. Her eldest daughter has two children, a girl and a boy. The girl shares my name and that of my mother—we call her Mattie—and the boy, already tall at only six, is named Robert after our grandfather.

I keep Mother's prized labyrinth trimmed, the hedges wide and evergreen. It's still possible to get lost in it and every week or so I hear the squeals and shouts of children begging for rescue, though the path to the quicksand was walled off last year, in 2000. Deep in the center of the labyrinth is a large stone, its inscription underscored by a single carved musical note: *Roderick and Jonathan Usher*.

I am the last of the Ushers. Being the last of a clan gives one a small power. With it, I embrace Jonathan and hold him within our walls. More than anyone he has captured our dream of Usher, its three stories lifted by the yearning of the violin and the cello, by the warmth of the piano's resonant tones, a place for the living and the dead, room for us all.

Acknowledgments

I want to thank Hilda Raz and Elisabeth Sharp McKetta for their enthusiasm and insights on many of these stories and for their guidance on arranging this collection. And a big thank-you to others in my critique group with whom I regularly write and discuss writing: Ruth Rudner and Sue Hallgarth. I'm also grateful to my irreverent generative writing group: Lynda Miller, Cynthia Sylvester, Harriet Lindenberg, Tanya Brown, and Ellen Barber—your laughter and creativity (and inventive prompts) encouraged the launching of so many of the stories in *The Lost Archive*. Thank you as well to early readers Laurie Hause, Bev Magennis, and Anne Cooper. I'm appreciative of my podcast partner on *The Unruly Muse*, John Modaff, for helping me hone some of these stories as we performed them together on our shows. Thanks also to Julie Williams for her excitement about and belief in these stories. All of you mentioned here are such wonderful writers and readers and listeners; you birth stories! A special shout-out to my wife, Lynda Miller, for her patience reading many drafts and her love of narrative.

I wish to credit the following journals for publishing the following stories:

An earlier version of "David's Harvest" appeared in the *North Dakota Quarterly* 65, no. 4 (1998).

"Words Shimmer," *Chautauqua Journal* 13 (2016).

"How Did You Know It Was Time to Go?," *Articulated Short Story Anthology* (2016).

"Pale Blue," *The Apple Valley Review* (Spring 2018).

"Afterthought," *The MacGuffin* (Winter 2019).

"Is It Really You?," Scribes Valley Publishing fiction anthology (2020).

"Noir by Night," *ABQ inPrint* 4 (Fall 2020).

"Pueblo Luna," *ABQ inPrint* 6 (Fall 2022).

Lynn C. Miller is the author of four novels. Her third novel, *The Day after Death*, was named a 2017 Lambda Literary Award finalist. Short plays and stories have appeared in various periodicals, including *Chautauqua Journal*, where the short story "Words Shimmer" was named runner-up for the Editors' Prize. She has performed and directed the work of many women writers, including Gertrude Stein, Edith Wharton, Victoria Woodhull, and Katherine Anne Porter, and sometimes weaves their histories into her writing. Miller taught performance studies and writing at the University of Southern California, the Pennsylvania State University, and the University of Texas at Austin, where she was a professor of theater and dance until 2007. She is copublisher of Bosque Press, cohost of the podcast *The Unruly Muse*, and lives in Los Ranchos, New Mexico. For more information, go to www.lynncmiller.com.